He walks...
he talks...
he kills.

Buffy
THE
VAMPIRE SLAYER™

D0034885

HALLOWEEN RAIN

Christopher Golden and Nancy Holder
Based on the hit TV series created by Joss Whedon

Check out the Buffy the Vampire
Slayer™ fan club at
www.buffyfanclub.com

INTO THE DARK . . .

Down Buffy went, listening to her own heartbeat. There was the mildew smell of standing water mixed with the smell of dirt and perfume. She heard low laughter.

Candlelight glowed against the wall as she reached the foot of the stairs. There was soft music playing. She reached the corner, paused for a heartbeat, then three. Finally, she poked her head out and saw four or five couples cuddling on some old couches draped with bedspreads. She hesitated. Maybe this was her cue to mutter, "Sorry," and tiptoe back upstairs. But she knew that something funky was going on. Something unnatural. Evil.

Then she heard the whimpering.

And the slurping.

Buffy turned on her flashlight and held it high above her head.

Five vampires, five human victims pinned beneath them on the couches. The vamps raised their faces and hissed at her. Blood glittered on their lips.

"Get her!" one of the vampires shouted, and they moved toward her as one, a wall of living darkness.

Upstairs, the door slammed shut.

Buffy, the Vampire Slayer™ books

#1 The Harvest
#2 Halloween Rain
#3 Coyote Moon (coming in mid-December)

Available from ARCHWAY Paperbacks

BUFFY THE·VAMPIRE SLAYER™

HALLOWEEN RAIN

Christopher Golden and Nancy Holder
Based on the hit TV series created by Joss Whedon

AN ARCHWAY PAPERBACK
Published by POCKET BOOKS
New York London Toronto Sydney Tokyo Singapore

AN ARCHWAY PAPERBACK *Original*

 An Archway Paperback published by
POCKET BOOKS, a division of Simon & Schuster Inc.
1230 Avenue of the Americas, New York, NY 10020

™ and copyright © 1997 by Twentieth Century Fox Film Corporation. All rights reserved.

ISBN: 0-671-01713-6

First Archway Paperback printing November 1997

10 9 8 7 6 5 4 3 2 1

AN ARCHWAY PAPERBACK and colophon are registered trademarks of Simon & Schuster Inc.

Printed in the U.S.A.

IL 7+

For Nancy,
who honored me with this collaboration,
and for Sarah Michelle Gellar,
who makes it all look so easy.

—C.G.

To my beloved daughter, Belle.
I hope you'll grow up to be as strong and brave as Buffy,
as clever as Willow,
and as silly as your dad.

To Chris, my wonderful coauthor. You're the greatest.

—N.H.

Acknowledgments

No novel is ever completed without a supporting cast and crew. Christopher Golden and Nancy Holder would like to thank the people who helped us with our excellent adventure in Buffy Land, AKA Boca del Infierno. They are: our agents, Lori Perkins and Howard Morhaim; Joss Whedon and everyone connected with our favorite Slayer, Sarah Michelle Gellar; our wonderful families, especially Connie and Wayne; and our Pocket posse, Lisa Clancy, Liz Shiflett, and Helena Santini. A thank-you, also, to Alice Alfonsi, for the jump-start.

And to Isabell Granados from Nancy, *muchas gracias*.

HALLOWEEN RAIN

PROLOGUE

It was getting late. In the dim moonlight, the statues atop the gravestones in the Sunnydale Cemetery cast strange shadow-shapes across the dark mounds under which the town's dead lay. How long they might stay buried was in question, of course, since Sunnydale had another name. Early Spanish settlers called it Boca del Infierno. Buffy Summers didn't need to *habla* to translate: she lived in the Hellmouth.

Literally.

The cemetery provided the clearest indication of the town's true nature. Weeping stone angels became laughing devils. Hands clasped in prayer looked like ripping claws. Crosses hung upside down.

Way boring.

Buffy the Vampire Slayer stood just outside the cemetery and scanned the darkness among the gravestones for trouble. She sighed heavily as she

1

leaned her elbows on the cemetery's granite wall. October 30th was almost over. She'd been out on patrol for hours, and she hadn't seen one vampire, one demon, one witch, one anything.

Well, okay, one witch. In gym. But Cordelia didn't count. She wasn't supernaturally evil. She only acted like a broom rider. Buffy understood. Poor Cordelia was cursed with popularity, great clothes, and, no lie, she was a babe. Naturally she had to take her frustrations out on everybody who didn't have it as good as she did.

Buffy supposed she should count her own blessings. She and Giles, her Watcher, had both expected the Halloween season to be the equivalent of finals for her Slayer diploma. All through October she'd trained hard, kept in shape, and sharpened up some very thick and sturdy pieces of wood. She was psyched for slaughter. She was pumped for pounding.

The little things a teenager gets excited about.

But now, standing outside the graveyard, the only monsters she was fighting were major Godzilla yawns. Buffy was so not thrilled. She hadn't seen any extreme vampire action for three weeks. Or much of anything else. Zip. Zilch. Nada. She'd been so bored she'd actually started to study. But that novelty was so over.

Still, no vamp sightings. Wasn't this cause for putting on a happy face?

Ever since she'd found out she was the Chosen One, all she'd wanted was to be a normal teenage girl. Maybe even a cheerleader. To have a honey of a boyfriend, hang out with her friends, and try to graduate from high school while doing as little actual studying as possible.

Instead, her extracurriculars centered around staking vampires, wasting monsters, and trying to keep her friends breathing long enough for them to graduate from high school. Much joy, what a treat. Smart, cute chick in desperate need of a life. But did she try to get a life? No, she wandered around looking for something undead to re-dead.

Pathetic much?

It isn't bad enough I have to pull the night shift, Buffy thought, *but how much more of a waste of time is it to be the Slayer when all the slayees are of town or something?*

"Yo, dead guys," she called mournfully. Then she shrugged. What the hell. Her mom would tell her not to look a gift horse in the mouth. Good symbolism: teeth were a big issue in Buffy's life. If you had long, sharp, pointy ones, she killed you.

Not tonight. She was a soldier without a war. All dressed up and no one to destroy. Time to call it a night, she figured. Maybe Willow would come over for some American history tutoring and they could scarf all the Halloween candy Buffy's mom had bought at the store. Or they could curl up with a good gory horror movie, the way Buffy and her mom used to do before Buffy had to burn down the gym at her old high school to kill a bunch of vampires, and they had to move to Sunnydale.

Out of the frying pan, into the mouth of hell.

From deep within the cemetery, a bloodcurdling scream pierced the night. Without hesitation, Buffy vaulted over the cemetery wall. She scanned left and right as she raced in the direction of the scream, dodging broken headstones, bushes, and tree roots. Just in case, she yanked open her shoulder bag and pulled out a stake. Boy Scouts and vampire slayers should always be prepared.

Another scream, this one louder and more frantic.

She ran faster, wondering what she would be going up against. One vampire? Two? A tribe of them? Or something she had never encountered before, a Halloween treat from hell? For half a second, she wished she had an elsewhere to be, but she brushed the thought away. She'd been looking for trouble. Now it had found her. She was the Chosen One, after all.

Another scream—shriek, more like. Now Buffy could tell it was a girl's voice. Screaming.

"Oh, God, stop!" it went on.

Afraid she might be too late, Buffy charged around the nearest headstone.

A blond-haired girl was struggling and kicking on the long, marble slab top of a tomb. A dark figure held both her wrists in his clutches, and he laughed and lowered his head, aiming for her neck. The girl shrieked even louder.

Buffy put one sneaker on top of a headstone and launched herself through the air. She tore the figure off the girl and they tumbled to the ground beside the tomb together. She threw him on his back, wrapped her hands around the stake, took aim, and—

"Stop!" the girl on the tomb screeched in abject terror. "Leave him alone!"

Buffy glanced up at the shadowed face of the girl's attacker. It was John Bartlett, who sat across from her in trig class. And his "victim" was Aphrodesia Kingsbury, his girlfriend.

"What's your *damage,* Buffy?" Aphrodesia yelled, as John scrabbled away from Buffy. Aphrodesia threw her arms around him. "Insane much? Are you, like, asylum bound or what?"

Buffy moved away from John, put the stake in her bag as calmly as she could, and cleared her throat. "Sorry," she muttered. "I, ah, thought you were someone else."

She got to her feet. The two kids stared at her. She tried to smile, her face twisted into a grimace of acute humiliation. "Sorry," she said again. "Ah, happy Halloween."

She turned around and squared her shoulders, walking back the way she had come with as much dignity as she could muster.

"What a psycho," Aphrodesia said, and didn't even bother to whisper.

"Way psycho," John replied. "She's a hotty, though."

"Jo-ohn!" Aphrodesia whined.

Buffy could hear them bickering all the way to the cemetery wall. It was that disgustingly sweet bickering people did when they actually had a someone to bicker with. Buffy the Chosen One, the Slayer, the complete moron, went home to concentrate on eating all the frozen yogurt in the house.

After all, tomorrow was another day. And another night.

Halloween night, actually.

And there had to be something to keep a Slayer busy on Halloween.

CHAPTER 1

Buffy hadn't slept well, and as if she wasn't tired enough already, the sky was crowded with dark clouds, the air heavy and damp with the threat of rain. It was the kind of day that just made you want to pull the covers over your head and snooze all day. Like a vampire. It was the kind of day when guys and gals too hip to get cancer got all broken up because they couldn't work on their tans.

Actually, sometimes Buffy thought it would be better if tans hadn't suddenly become as uncool as smoking. It'd be a lot easier to tell the undead from the brain dead.

Resolved to stay awake in first period, she forced her eyes open wider. Backpack over her shoulder, Buffy marched toward school, a little early as always. Well, not always. She was never even on time at her old school, but she was trying to reform. And be-

7

sides, when she showed early, she got to hang with Willow and Xander for a few minutes before the whole grand delirium of the school day began.

"Happy Halloween!" Xander cried as he caught up from behind.

Buffy smiled slightly as he fell into step with her. "Xander, isn't Halloween, like, prom night for ghouls? The night when, all over the world, the forces of darkness are set free for their annual block party?"

"Well, yeah, but it's all costumes and parties and trick-or-treat and—" Xander began, but Buffy cut him off.

"And where do we live?" she prodded.

"Okay, I get the point," he surrendered. "But things have been pretty quiet lately, so I figured, why not be a little festive during my used-to-be-favorite-before-I-knew-all-this-stuff-was-real holiday?"

Buffy gave up. "Happy Halloween to you, too, Xander." She winced inside. The last person she'd offered season's greetings to had called her a thundering psycho.

Xander Harris offered her a charming, crooked smile and pushed his somebody-get-me-a-comb hair away from his forehead. It seemed as if he wanted to say something more, but by then they had reached the bench where they met each morning. Willow was already there, her nose in a huge, dusty old book. The title was something about arcane rituals.

Xander peered over her shoulder. "Willow, dear

Willow, you used to read such wholesome things." He feigned almost parental disapproval. "Now you've just fallen in with the wrong crowd."

Willow closed her book. "Giles loaned it to me," she said. "Fascinating stuff, actually. Apparently, there was this sixteenth-century alchemist who— and you guys really don't want to hear this anyway."

Buffy and Xander exchanged innocent looks— Who, us? Not enraptured? But it would be a cold day in a place like, well, here, when they could put anything over on her. She tutored both of them in different subjects, was an Internet commando, and once in a while had to serve as Giles's translator, when the stuffy British librarian forgot he was speaking to people who hadn't spent their entire lives locked up in the Twilight Zone library.

"Happy Halloween, Willow," Buffy said warmly.

"Yeah, trick or treat, *chica,*" Xander added.

With her long, straight chestnut hair and sad eyes, Willow Rosenberg was every bit as sweet yet, um, unelegant, as her name might suggest. But she and Xander were the best friends Buffy had ever had. They knew everything about her, about her being the Slayer, and they stuck by her. In fact, time and again, Willow and Xander put their lives on the line for her, and for the town.

Buffy was the Chosen One. Slaying was her job. Willow and Xander did all the crazy stuff by choice. As far as Buffy was concerned, her friends were a lot braver than they ever gave themselves credit for.

"I don't know," Willow said, as Buffy and Xander sat on the bench on either side of her. "Halloween isn't a big deal anymore. I mean, when we were kids, we got to dress up and go trick-or-treating. Once you're in the double digits, it's so over. I think I'm in mourning for my childhood, and I'm only sixteen."

"Clone that," Buffy said.

"Remember bobbing for apples at those killer Halloween parties your mom used to throw?" Xander asked Willow, and she smiled at him.

The two had known each other their whole lives, and Buffy had only come along this year. But they never made her feel left out, even when they talked about things they'd shared in the past.

"I remember you trying to drown me while I was bobbing for apples," Willow replied, then turned to Buffy. "It's amazing the selective memory guys have."

"Well, you know guys only tease girls when they're trying to get noticed," Buffy said, and raised an eyebrow.

"I noticed him when I was, like, five years old," Willow said under her breath. "I'm waiting for him to notice I noticed."

"I loved those parties," Xander went on, oblivious to Willow's comments. "I always used to win the pumpkin-carving contest. Big fun."

He sighed. "You're right. Halloween sucks now. Even the horror movies on cable aren't as fun anymore, ever since . . ." He hesitated. "Ah, ever since—"

"I know," Buffy said, sighing. "Ever since I came to town. I feel the same way. My mother and I used to watch all the classic fright flicks together and gorge ourselves on popcorn and leftover Halloween candy. Somehow I've lost interest in the movies. Now we just gorge ourselves."

Buffy felt a drop of rain on her arm and was about to mention it when Willow tapped her leg.

"Wicked witch and winged monkeys at ten o'clock," she murmured.

Buffy looked up to see Cordelia and her fan club about to pass by. Cordelia paid no attention to them, but Aphrodesia Kingsbury was with her, and Buffy glanced away as the girl spotted her.

"Well, if it isn't my stalker," Aphrodesia sneered. "I told them all about it, Buffy, so don't try to deny your after-hours bipolar wig out to anyone on campus." She glared at her. "Isn't there some kind of medication you're forgetting to take?"

Before Buffy could respond, Xander snapped angrily, "Careful, Miss twenty-five-watt. I wouldn't make Buffy mad if I were you."

"Xander," Buffy hissed, and Willow elbowed him in the stomach.

"Excuse me? Are you threatening me?" Aphrodesia said, zooming in like a heat-seeking missile on Xander. "Because my sister's fiancé is in law school and, like, he told me he would serve anybody I asked him to."

"You know, I'd love it if he served me. I can't seem to get my own waiter's attention and we don't even have menus yet," Xander mocked. "Good help. Hard to find. So."

"Oh, you people are so . . . *not,*" Aphrodesia said, wrinkling her nose as if she'd smelled something nasty. "You two." She nodded toward Xander and Willow. "It's like Cordelia says. You're just run-of-the-mill losers. With a lot of effort, you might actually evolve into primates. But not if you loiter with Buffy. Her weirdness is like some brain-eating virus, and it's seriously infected your chances for a normal social life."

By then, Cordelia and the rest of her crew had moved on, and Aphrodesia spun in a huff to follow.

"Y'know, I've seen *Heathers,*" Buffy said aloud. "I just want to know why Christian Slater is never around when you need him."

The three of them were quiet until the others were out of earshot. Then Willow turned to Xander with her eyebrows raised.

"What?" Xander asked.

"Miss twenty-five-watt?"

"Well, Aphrodesia's not very bright," Xander explained. "Twenty-five-watt. Get it?"

"Got it," Buffy and Willow said simultaneously.

"Who writes your stuff?" Buffy asked, and the girls laughed together.

"Well, I thought it was funny," Xander mumbled snippily.

"We're just kidding, Xander," Willow said. "You know we love you."

"Good thing, or you'd both be in deep can't-say-that-on-television," he replied menacingly.

"Witness our trembling," Buffy drawled.

"I have that effect on women," Xander announced.

"So," Willow said, "you guys both coming to the Bronze tonight?"

"The masquerade! Wouldn't miss it!" Xander said excitedly. "I'm going as Indiana Jones."

"Oh, I'm so not surprised," Willow said. "You've dressed in that stupid hat every Halloween since you were nine."

Xander stared at her, horrified, and Buffy stifled a laugh to save him from further embarrassment.

"If adventure has a name, my dear, it's Xander Harris," he said proudly. "Well, actually, it's Harrison Ford, but women confuse the two of us all the time."

They stared at him.

"Okay, it's happened a couple of times . . . once . . . okay, never, but we have kind of the same hair color," Xander explained. "Brown. And my mom thinks I look like him. I suppose you two have a better costume idea for me?"

"I've got one, but I'll tell you later," Willow said cryptically. "It's a surprise for Buffy."

"For me? I'm an extreme no-show tonight," Buffy protested. "It's the Slayer Superbowl."

Willow and Xander both frowned at her. For once, no snappy retorts. She was almost insulted, but then realized their silence was skeptical comment enough. Both of them knew that she'd been bored out of her mind the past few weeks.

"Okay, I am majorly sorry to have to blink and miss the masquerade, and I know you fun seekers think I'm so wasting my time, but it's Halloween night," Buffy explained. "I mean, so business has been a little slow—"

"Way slow," Willow corrected.

"Way slow," Buffy agreed. "But it's got to pick up tonight."

"You sound like you want it to pick up tonight," Xander said. "I know compared to L.A. raves, a masquerade is tiny potatoes. But trust us, it's the most fun you can have in this agonizingly mall-less town."

"Come on, Buffy," Willow pleaded. "At least you can start out at the Bronze. If there's a gory emergency you can always book."

Buffy thought about it, but not for long. If she didn't start hanging with her friends more, they might adopt a new Slayer as their bud. Or not, since there weren't any others. One in every generation, that was Giles's favorite part of the Big Book of Slayage. But she still liked the idea of a quiet night at the Bronze.

"I'll talk to Giles," Buffy decided. "He still thinks this is all just the calm before the storm."

"Tell him we'll take care of you," Xander suggested.

"Yeah, I'll carry your bag o' holy water and Xander will gas up the Batmobile," Willow said.

As soon as the freedom bell rang, announcing that school was mercifully over for another day, Buffy was up and fighting through the swarm. In the hall, lockers clanged, gossip raged, girls shrieked, and guys laughed. She heard snippets of conversation, mostly about what people were wearing to the masquerade. There was mischief in the air, and a sense that anyone could burst into a fit of the giggles at any time. Halloween was such a kids' holiday.

But it hadn't always been that way. Giles was up on all the wicked history, but Buffy knew enough of it to know Halloween was made up to replace some kind of ancient death ritual or something. She'd have to ask him. Actually, come to think of it, she probably wouldn't have to ask him. Giles didn't usually need to be asked to start lecturing. He just did.

The hall traffic had started to thin. Buffy blew off her locker; she had everything she needed for the weekend in her backpack. Instead, she headed for the library to check in with Giles.

Buffy was passing by the science lab when powerful hands with matted fur and yellow claws flashed out and snagged her by the shoulders. Out of the corner of her eye she saw the open jaws of the werewolf and reacted: a hard elbow to the ribs met with a satisfying grunt from behind. There was a roar in front of her, and Buffy looked up to see a second werewolf approaching. She straight-armed this one with the flat of her hand, knocking him on his butt, leaping high into an aerial roundhouse kick while her brain struggled frantically to send her a message: *Cease. Desist. Remember the graveyard, Buffy?*

Buffy pulled back on the kick and landed ungracefully on her behind. She glanced at the two "werewolves," whom she now realized were just big guys in full costume.

"Way to go, Jackie Chan," a short guy with thick glasses and a leaning tower of books cried happily. "Those guys have been defining obnoxious with their bad-hair-scare tactics."

"Uh, sorry," she mumbled to the nearer one, who was trying to get to his knees. The other one was using all the words that were still forbidden in chat rooms and on sitcoms. "Your costumes are, ah, really there. I guess I'm just a little jumpy."

Buffy looked up in time to see the gathering crowd of vultures part for their queen, Cordelia, and her entourage. Before the other girl swooped down for the attack, Buffy winced and tiredly rolled her eyes.

"Jumpy?" Cordelia parroted. "Just a little psycho, more like. Guys, take note, a major body lingo signal from Buffy here. Don't invade her personal space or she'll go all, like, special forces on you. Or maybe you thought they were real werewolves, huh, Summers?"

"Never know what's going to pop its ugly monster

Pez-head up out of hell on Halloween, Cordelia. Witness your sudden arrival," Buffy snapped, then spun and stalked away toward the library. She could almost hear the anger building inside Cordelia Chase.

"Bye-bye, Buffy the walking X-file," Cordelia called after her, followed by a chorus of laughter from kids without the guts to make fun of her to her face.

If she cared about fitting in, if she allowed her feelings to be hurt by someone as deep as the kiddie pool, she might have been upset. But Buffy was so above it all. She was the Slayer. Normal teen angst didn't stack up to fangs at your throat.

Sometimes, it was worse.

Sure, she was the Slayer, but Buffy's face was flushed and she couldn't have forced a smile onto her face with a Neiman Marcus shopping spree. Well, maybe that. She did need black boots. And a few other things.

When she pulled open the door to the library, Buffy was smiling again and thinking cashmere. Winter was coming after all. Cordelia's tongue was a weapon, but her hack-and-slash approach was clumsy enough that the wounds were never deep.

At a long research table in the library was a stack of moldy old books that could only belong to one man. But despite the presence of titles like *Archaic Druidry, Celtic Magick,* and *Shadow Realms,* among many others, their owner was nowhere in sight.

"Giles?" Buffy called.

"Hmm?" a mumbled response came from the library second-story loft. "Oh, yes, Buffy, up here. Is school over already, or are you cutting class again?"

She looked up at him, and realized Giles hadn't even taken his eyes off the racks of books.

"The school is burning down, Giles," she said, trying to raise some reaction. Nothing. "You didn't even hear the bell. What's got you by the nostrils?"

No response.

"Giles?"

"Sorry," he said, distracted. "I'll be down in a moment."

Buffy slid her backpack onto the table. She dropped into a chair, leaned back, and planted her feet on the scarred oak. A quick glance around told her something she'd already known; she and Giles were alone in the library.

Of course they were. Even before Rupert Giles left the staff of the British Museum to become school librarian at Sunnydale High—a career move roughly equivalent to an appointment with Dr. Kevorkian—the library wasn't exactly the place to be seen by people hip enough to look. It was more like a dungeon with books, and barely enough light to read them by.

Still was. Only now, it was *Mission: Impossible* to find the books kids actually needed for class. Giles had brought in his own collection, so very not the kind of reading material parents wanted their college-bound spawn to lay paws on. The librarian had more important things to worry about. He was the Watcher. His job was to prepare the Slayer for her work, to train and educate her, to teach her what she needed to know to keep breathing.

A bit of a stiff, but Giles was all right in Buffy's book. His job was keeping her alive, after all. How bad could the guy be? Call a press conference, though, she actually liked him. He was kind of absent-minded, and talked way British—she could hardly understand him at times—but he was cool. Handsome, too, in that your-dad's-pretty-good-looking-for-an-old-guy kind of way.

Buffy just wished he wouldn't get all overprotective so often. She had a hard enough time getting her mother to let her have a life.

The library door swung open, and Buffy started and spun to face the door. It was only Willow and Xander, though, and she relaxed immediately.

"Not too jumpy, are we?" Xander asked.

"See, that's what I told Cordelia," Buffy said, and smiled.

"We heard," Willow admitted. "Good thing you didn't try beheading those impostor-monsters."

"There's always next time," Buffy replied with a shrug.

Giles came down the stairs behind them, and they all turned to see him fumbling with a tall stack of books in his arms. Buffy held her breath until he reached the bottom, afraid he was going to trip any second. But Giles made it to the table without disaster.

"Ah," he said as he glanced around at them.

"You're all here. Excellent. I'm in the middle of an important research project, but I want to give you a bit of preparation for Halloween. Buffy's heard most of this, but as tonight *is* Halloween, I thought perhaps this time she might actually pay attention."

Buffy shot Giles a withering glance, but he went on, totally unwithered. She didn't argue, though. She hadn't really paid attention before.

"Whoa, camel," Xander interrupted. "We've got this masquerade at the Bronze tonight. Didn't Buffy tell you?"

"Tell me?" Giles asked. "Tell me what?"

"I'm off duty tonight," Buffy declared. "It's been way dead in the undead department, boss. I figure it can't hurt to pretend Halloween's just tricks and treats."

"First of all, Buffy, I am not your boss," Giles huffed. "Your mentor, perhaps, if you would do me the honor of considering me such. But not boss. You are the Slayer, and I the Watcher. Secondly, I'm afraid what you propose is impossible."

"She didn't propose," Willow said. "I didn't hear her proposing."

"Definite no proposing," Xander agreed. "More of an announcement. Attention K-Mart shoppers, no slaying tonight. That kind of thing."

Giles sighed deeply.

"You must understand, all of you," he began. "The recent lull in supernatural activity, vampiric or otherwise, does not necessarily mean that tonight will be as quiet as we would all wish. To understand, you must understand Halloween itself."

"Here he goes," Buffy said, and rolled her eyes.

"In Celtic times," Giles explained, "the year began in February and lasted until late October. The winter months, during which the land would wither and die, weren't even considered real time, in a sense, but a barren world of shadow and worship of the dark gods, what we call demons, or ancient ones.

"During this dead time, called Samhuinn, the gates between worlds were open, the dead and the living could mingle. There were feasts for the dead, bribes for the evil ones among them, offerings to convince them not to harm the innocent and rituals to keep them bound.

"Over time, as the faith in such things has waned, the season has shortened so that it now lasts only three days, from today, October thirty-first, to the second of November. But tonight is the night when the Druid priests would hold the ceremony marking the beginning of Samhuinn, and the night when the tribes of the night run free. Without the rituals and offerings to control them, the evil ones are not kept at bay.

"When the English Christians converted the Celts, they changed the names of these days. October thirty-first became All Hallow's Eve, or Hallowe'en," Giles concluded, then took a breath and looked at them expectantly.

The three teens stared back.

"So your point would be what?" Xander asked.

Giles pushed his glasses up his nose and looked at the Slayer. "Buffy?" he asked.

Buffy sighed. "His extreme boredom point would be that whatever happened up until tonight meant as much as a political promise," she explained. "Tonight the dead pull a Pinky and the Brain, and try to take over the world."

Xander and Willow stared at Buffy, then glanced at Giles before meeting each other's gaze. Finally, Xander said, "Willow, are you pondering what I'm pondering?"

"Yes, Xander. Indeed," Willow replied, then looked at Buffy and Giles as if they'd flunked kindergarten.

"Maybe I just haven't been, y'know, paying attention," she said. "But why hasn't this happened before? Okay, since Buffy's been here, things have gotten weirder, but Sunnydale is at the mouth of hell, remember. If Halloween was all that, wouldn't the whole town have been dusted decades ago?"

"Well," Giles replied, "there is that."

"Wait," Buffy said. "You just said since nobody believes in these guys anymore, Halloween keeps shrinking, right?"

"Something like that," Giles admitted.

"I get it," Xander said. "So, this Samhuinn thing is just . . . over, right?"

"*So* over," Buffy agreed. "Which means a quiet night, which means I am going to the masquerade."

Giles began to clear his throat. The stern expression on his face made it clear he was not with Buffy's program at all. She decided quickly that a compromise was in order.

"Okay, plea bargain time," she said. "I'll only stay for a while, then I'll go out and have a look around. If it's still quiet, I'll go back to the party. If there's slaying to be done, well, I'm the Slayer. Deal?"

"What choice do I have?" Giles moaned. "As you say, you are the Slayer."

"Right," Buffy said happily. "I keep forgetting that part."

"Cool," Xander said. "Just make sure you stay clear of farms and fields, anywhere there's a scarecrow."

Buffy frowned. "Or a tin man or a lion?" she asked.

"It's raining today, duh!" Xander said, then slapped himself in the forehead. "Duh again! You're not from around here."

Buffy looked at Willow. "What flight is he on?" she asked with very mild annoyance.

"It's a local thing, kind of a bogeyman-type legend," Willow explained. "According to the stories, there's dark magic in Halloween rain. If it soaks into a scarecrow, and you trespass on the scarecrow's territory, it will come to life and give you a stern talking to. No, extreme punishment, really."

"Odd," Giles said. "I've never even heard such a legend, and yet there are many references to a tie between scarecrows and Samhain."

"Samhuinn again?" Xander asked.

"Not quite the same thing," Giles explained.

"Samhuinn is the season or the night of ritual itself. Samhain is the spirit of Hallowe'en, the king of the dead souls who haunted the land of the living on that night. Apparently, he was one of the demons, one of the ancient ones who inhabited this world before the birth of humanity, and he was sort of adopted by the Celts as one of their gods."

"So he's a foster demon, really," Xander joked.

"Not a laughing matter," Giles said, turning to the stack of books he'd brought down. "Samhain is one of the most evil creatures ever to walk the earth. Vicious and cunning. I really ought to look into this . . ."

The Watcher's words trailed off as he lost himself in his books again.

Buffy, Xander, and Willow waited for a few seconds, to see if Giles would continue. He didn't. The books had possessed him again, and the rest of them had become invisible.

Finally, Buffy shrugged.

"So, see you tonight," she said to Willow and Xander. "Watch out for wet scarecrows."

"It's no joke, Buffy," Xander said.

"Who's joking?" Buffy asked.

CHAPTER 2

When Buffy bounced down the last couple of stairs toward the living room, she could hear the popcorn drum solo coming from the microwave. The smell started her craving salt, butter, and those little unpopped kernels she always gagged on. Her mom sat in the living room watching *Fright Night* on Showtime. Buffy smiled. Mom had no idea she was watching what amounted to Slayer training videos.

After she'd gone into the kitchen and dumped the popcorn into a large bowl, Buffy went in to see her mother. She slid the bowl onto the coffee table and stood and watched the movie for a moment.

"Sit down, honey," her mother said without looking up. "After this, they're going to show *Burnt Offerings*. Now that's a creepy one."

"Uh, I'd really love to, Mom, but I'm supposed to

meet Willow and Xander down at the Bronze. There's a masquerade tonight," Buffy said quickly.

Her mother had glanced up as she spoke, and Buffy could see the surprise and then disappointment in her eyes as Joyce Summers saw that her daughter was in costume, and then realized what that meant. Then the disappointment evaporated.

"That's great, Buffy," Joyce said. "I guess I can't complain when you hang out with that Willow. She's a nice girl. I'd like to know more about this boy Xander though."

"*So* nothing there, Mom," Buffy said, rolling her eyes. "Sorry to dash your hopes against the rocks of my singleness, but he's just a friend."

"Well, I'm sure your singleness will be in jeopardy once you show up at the Bronze in that costume," her mother replied with a mixture of teasing and disapproval. "It's a bit . . . abbreviated."

Of course her mother had no idea that this year, Buffy had dressed for function and not form: in her knee boots, black shorts, and red silk blouse tied in a knot, the Chosen One could leap, kick, gouge, run, and skewer with the greatest of ease. Add a patch over one eye—yo, ho, ho and a bottle of root beer. If anybody asked, she was captain of the H.M.S. *Hellmouth*. The very model of a modern Slayer general.

"I'm a pirate queen, Mom," Buffy explained. "Like Anne Bonny. They all dressed like this."

"I don't know about that," her mother commented. "Just please be careful. You don't want to attract the wrong kind of attention."

Of course not, Buffy thought. No slavering six-teen-year-old boys, just slavering, long-fanged vam-pires.

Major sigh.

Her mother had offered to drive her to the Bronze, but Buffy just couldn't accept. If there was trouble, it would be easier for her to handle knowing her mom was safe at home where no uninvited vampires could cross their threshold. Not to mention that when your reputation needed CPR, you might as well show up in a hearse as have your parents drive you somewhere.

Still, she knew it was no joy for her mom to be alone in a new town on a nostalgic night, and Buffy was sorry.

Things were quiet on the walk. Buffy scanned the area through her clear plastic umbrella, seeing noth-ing but glowing pumpkin faces on porches, the moon shrouded by clouds, and her own shadow splashed across buildings like a billboard: *Here she is! The Slayer, all alone!* But no one was checking the classifieds, not a single vampire or demon, and definitely no walking scarecrows. Come to think of it, she couldn't remember if she'd ever seen a scarecrow in Sunnydale. There were some fields by the cemetery, but she couldn't recall any straw men hanging around. It would be a long detour to the Bronze just to go over there and cross them off her sightseeing list. Another time, she thought.

By the time Buffy got to the Bronze, the rain had slowed but not stopped. She paid the cover to the masked hunchback at the door and joined the rest of the crowd streaming inside.

Xander and Willow had been right: on Halloween night, the Bronze was clearly the place to be if you were too old to beg for candy from strangers. Sunken cheek by devil tail, the club was jammed with dozens of witches, Frankenstein monsters and Count Draculas, four zombies, three mad scientists, two white-sheeted ghosts, and a hanged man in a pear tree.

Everyone was a little damp from the rain, and through the Bronze wafted a fragrance that could only be called eau de wet dog. Makeup was running, frizzed-out Bride of Frankenstein hair was sagging, and costumes were clinging conspicuously to people who possessed any conspicuosities to be clung to. Hey, not everybody at sixteen looked like Wonderbra Woman.

Speaking of possessed, Cordelia was in the corner putting the hex on some honey wearing a buckskin shirt, chaps, and moccasins. Cordelia was working overtime for tepee time in a very slinky, clingy Morticia Addams unoriginal complemented by her natural black hair, matching lips, nails, and soul. She had put a lot of time and no doubt somebody else's effort into the Spider Woman motif.

As Buffy looked on, Cordelia and the victim of her attentions were interrupted by a tall, dark stranger. He wore a white half-face Phantom of the Opera mask, and a long cloak, and Buffy thought that with his high cheekbones and shoulder-length, blue-black hair he looked Native American. The Phantom sneered something at the guy dressed up as an Indian. It looked as though the costume had pissed the Phantom off, because he got in threateningly close—Listerine close—and sneered something at the object of Cordelia's affections.

The costumed Indian backed off as if the Phantom were for real. Buffy watched him scramble away, obviously wigged. Then she stared in disgust as Cordelia shamelessly smiled at the Phantom, laid a hand on his biceps, and started chatting him up, herding him toward the bar.

"Major harlot," Buffy muttered under her breath, then turned to scan the rest of the masquerade.

Cardboard skeletons hung from the ceiling of the Bronze and each table was decorated with a black candle inside a grinning plastic jack-o'-lantern. Drinks spewing dry ice were lined up on tables and along the balcony railing. A fog machine churned out graveyard mist. The cover band jammed out a harsh version of Michael Jackson's "Thriller." Everybody was hopping at the zombie jamboree.

Willow and Xander weren't there yet. Buffy was less than eager to wait by herself. She was fast becoming the school psycho, just as she had been back at Hemery High in Los Angeles. She'd totally been there, had so done that. Giles would never savvy why she thought it was so not fair. All Superman had to do was put on a pair of glasses and act clumsy at his day job. He never had to contend with the evil forces of high school while trying to save the world.

"Buffy," Willow said behind her. Finally. "Hi."

Wedging herself against a couple of jock types dressed as girls, Buffy twisted herself around in a tight half circle to face Willow. Xander stood beside her. Buffy blinked.

Willow and Xander were wearing suits.

Xander's hair was slicked back. He was a new Xander, a Bizarro-world Xander, too young to be a yuppie and too clean-cut to be himself.

Willow was in a baggy dark blue suit with a skirt that hung down to her low heels. Oddly, her hair gleamed with a henna wash, and it looked pretty good. But as if to cancel out the color's cool factor, she had tied it back with a severe tortoise-shell clip.

"Accountants. How unique," Buffy said brightly. "I wish I'd thought of that. I could be scoring major babe points as we speak."

Willow frowned. "No, Buffy. Not accountants."

Xander looked dashed. "Scully and Mulder. *The X-Files.*" He flashed her a badge that read Sunnydale Junior Policeman and muttered, "FBI. You're under arrest for killing dead guys."

Buffy laughed. "It's perfect! I'm not exhibiting much originality, I fear. Just a pirate queen." She posed. "You two slap the cuffs on and I'll run 'em through."

"Oh, you look totally . . . seaworthy," Xander gushed.

Willow added, "I thought you might dress up like a vampire. You know, as a joke."

"Too self-referential. Besides, if I screwed up the uniform I might piss 'em off."

"Off-pissing of vampires. You'd never want to do that." Willow touched her hair a little shyly. "So, how do I look as a redhead?"

"A hotty," Buffy assured her. "Maybe you should keep it."

Xander looked confused as he glanced at Willow. "You did something to your hair?"

Willow and Buffy traded glances and looked back at him. Willow looked philosophical and said, "No, Xander. I've always had red hair."

"It, um, looks nice." He flushed and said to Buffy, "Well, I was hoping we'd finally get to see your secret Slayer costume."

Buffy shrugged. "Oh, I was going to wear it, but it's so hard to accessorize a skin-tight leotard. As I'm sure you know, Xander."

Xander threw back his head. "Yeah, but I had to hang up my cape. I was always getting typecast as a lovable, decent guy girls were safe around. Not that I'm not," he added quickly. Reconsidered. "Or that I am."

A man of the nineties, Buffy thought, *Xander seems totally confused about the acceptable male aggression level.*

"I am what I am," Willow said, "and that's all what I am."

Buffy nodded. It must be nice to be able to say that.

Ten times fast.

She gestured at the stage, bobbed her head in time to the backbeat. "The band is called?"

Willow smiled. "Children of the Night, believe it or not."

Buffy grinned and continued to rock with the rhythm. "What music they make," she said happily.

Xander kept glancing at Willow's hair, and now he piped up, as if he had finally made all the connections. "Willow," he said exuberantly. "Hair. Red. Red is good. Fire engines are red. Porsches are red."

"So is blood," said a deep, not-good voice.

Buffy's mouth dropped open. Shoulder to shoulder, hip to hip, a cold-flesh-and-congealed-blood vampire bumped into her as he carried a cup across the club.

"All right. Hold it right there and let's take it outside," Buffy said between gritted teeth, grabbing his arm.

"Please." He took a step backward, shaking her off.

A plague victim groused, "Ouch. That's my foot, dude."

The vampire ignored him. It was nearly the millennium, Buffy observed. These days, most people who still said dude got ignored.

"This is sacred Samhuinn, the night all demons run free," the vampire said.

"He read the same book as Rupert," Xander commented.

"A very sacred, holy night," the vampire continued, "when we rest while the others hunt."

"We being the fat cats?" Buffy jibed. "The ones who've ordered in?"

"The vampires." He said the word with dignity and pride, the way an armchair quarterback might say MVP or Cordelia might say holder of a platinum charge card.

"What? You sucky boys have the night off? No preying or slaying?" Buffy cocked her head and put her hand on the zipper of her Slayer's bag, which was sitting on a bar stool. In case he was hungry, she had a nice juicy stake just waiting for him. "But if this is a scared—sacred—holy night, shouldn't you be doing that whole praying thing in some church? Like, down in the tunnels with Big Daddy?"

"You mock us." The vampire narrowed his eyes. "You know that if it hadn't been for that earthquake, my master would not be trapped inside that buried church." He was speaking of his leader, the Master vampire who had emigrated to America with the thought of making it big, like so many others in the brave New World. He came to the Hellmouth for the purpose of opening a dimensional portal that would release a Pandora's box of evils into the world . . . including his followers.

That was a tricky business in itself; add in a major earthquake that tumbled him into a church and scattered the portal into pieces, and you have one very not-so-happy monster.

"Were it not for the unforeseen shaking of the earth, he would be above ground with us, here, now. We'd rule this place."

"The Bronze?" She looked around the room and spotted another fanged wonder. Another. Another. Once you noticed them, they stuck out like Waldo. The place was a regular Fangoria. "And you're here why? To measure for curtains?"

He flashed his nasty overbite at her and said, dead seriously, "We're here to have fun, the same as you."

"My idea of fun doesn't include ripping people's throats open and drinking their blood." Buffy opened the zipper of the bag and put her fingers around her cross, which she had taken off because it didn't go with her costume.

Stupid much?

The vampire offered her an evil smile. He lifted up a plastic cup. "You should try it sometime."

Willow covered her mouth. "There's human blood in there? Oh, God, I'm going to be sick."

Buffy raised her chin. "Anyone I know?"

"Just a snack." The vampire made a show of tipping back the cup and taking a good, long swallow. "Mmm. A fine bouquet. Young. Fresh. Innocent."

"So it's not Cordelia." Her hand hidden inside the

bag, Buffy gripped the stake and glared at the vampire. "If we were alone—"

"But we're not." He set the cup on the table next to the pumpkin candle and dabbed at his lips with his fingertips. "Truly. We're simply here for the celebration. I propose we call a truce."

"Which you'll break the first chance you get." Buffy took a step toward him. This time he did not back up.

"We won't break it," he said confidently. "You have my assurance."

"I'm supposed to stake our lives on your word?"

"Pun intended," Willow added, stepping up behind Buffy, then taking a very courageous step to the left, slightly away from her.

The vampire's smile was a cry for dental coverage with all major medical plans. "Tonight you can make fools of yourselves. Tomorrow night, we'll kill you."

"And my little dog, too?" Buffy sneered at him. "Don't count on it."

The vampire touched his cheap-hussy fingernail to his forehead in a kind of salute. "Oh, but we do. We count on it very much."

"Well, I'm counting now. As in, hike-taking is your best bet for surviving the night. Ten, nine, eight, seven, six—"

"Don't threaten me," the vampire said angrily. "Or I'll—"

"Hurt me?" Buffy flung at him. "Rip me to pieces? So much for your word."

The vampire growled and stomped away.

"Yeah, and don't come back." Xander doubled his fists.

"Have a Zen moment, Xander. I'm the Slayer. You, not so much."

Buffy patted his arm, touched by how her friends rallied to her defense. She was once again perplexed by the complex rules of high school life, where kids like these were outcasts while the cruelly hip had licenses to crush.

"We'll hope for the best, okay?" she said. "Try to have fun."

Xander lit up. "My wish is your command, O slaying one. Care to dance?"

Willow gave her a half-crooked smile and a shrug: Go ahead.

Buffy had picked up the vampire's cup and was looking into it. "There's nothing in this cup," she said. "He was toying with us."

"Buffy?" Xander pumped his arms in a vaguely disco manner. "Um, dancing?"

"You have got to be kidding," Buffy said slowly, as she stared at a couple across the room.

"Gee. No also works," Xander said, hurt.

"What? Oh, Xander, I didn't mean you," Buffy said. She pointed. "That's Jean-Luc Picard, the foreign exchange student." Actually, his name was Jean-Pierre Goddard, but no one got out of high school without a nickname. "And look who he's with."

"You've never been into the gossip thing before," Xander said.

"I'm looking," Willow announced. "Nothing I see is taking my breath away."

"He's with a vampire chick," Buffy announced, taking off her eye patch. Without turning her head, she felt for, and found, her Slayer satchel. "Looks like they're headed for the storage basement."

Indeed, the vamp chick, truly beautiful in a skimpy Cleopatra costume, had him by the nose— or rather, the hand—and she was letting her hips do the walking as the couple edged through the crowd. The look on Jean-Pierre's face spoke of the hope that he was going where no French foreign exchange student had gone before, and it wasn't to take inventory of how many black plastic cups the Bronze had on hand for the masquerade.

"How do you know she's a vampire?" Willow asked, with true curiosity. "I can't tell."

"Yeah, you wouldn't want to make a mistake and mess up a beautiful moment," Xander said.

Buffy shrugged. "Giles has been teaching me. There are a few clues. She's very pale. Her way of walking indicates she's a predator."

"Well, so is Cordelia, and if we staked her, we'd get in *mucho* big trouble," Xander pointed out.

"Or a medal," Willow said. She shivered. "What are you going to do, Buffy?"

"Mess up a beautiful moment. Hopefully, it won't be too messy."

"We'll come with," Xander announced.

"No way. You stay up here. Monitor the sitch. Make sure no one else follows." Buffy took a breath. Halloween was heating up after all. "For all I know, this is a plan to get me down there."

"Then don't go," Willow said nervously. "He's a big boy. He'll be able to fight her off."

Buffy grinned at Willow. "You know I can't do that. I have a solemn responsibility." She raised her chin and affected a British accent. "I and I alone, in all my generation, am the Slayah."

"Pip, pip," Xander said sourly. "Some girls will do anything to avoid dancing with me."

"Not all girls," Willow murmured.

"Yeah, well, enough of them."

"Dancing would be good," Buffy said. "You guys could funk n' roll over to the top of the basement stairs and stand guard."

"Well, if you put it that way, I guess sacrifices have to be made," Willow said. She firmly took Xander's hand and led him into the gyrating cast of thousands.

Buffy worked around the perimeter, muttering half-hearted excuse me's as she kept her gaze solidly on the storage door. It closed behind Jean-Pierre. She hurried, getting some protests as she bumped drink cups and stepped on toes. Couldn't be helped.

When she reached the door, she held her satchel between her knees and fastened her cross around her neck. In this crowd, flashing it sooner would be like flashing a sheriff's badge: Okay, ya lousy vampires, there's gonna be trouble. She wondered if all the really cool fangy people there knew the Slayer was in their midst. If there were wanted posters of her. If the Master did an orientation for new vampires that included a manila folder labeled Buffy Summers, Slayer. Dossier. Bloodshot eyes only.

Buffy opened the door.

The stairs went down at a sharp angle. Overhead, a bare light bulb hanging from the canted ceiling had burned out . . . or been smashed. She couldn't do anything about that unless she wanted to announce her approach. Same thing with turning on the hefty black flashlight in her bag.

She took the steps one at a time, moving as silently as fog.

Down she went, listening to her own heartbeat. Sparing a worry for her friends, even a thought for the French kid she'd never spoken to but was risking her life to protect.

Farther down.

There was the mildew smell of standing water mixed with the smell of dirt and perfume.

She heard low laughter.

Candlelight glowed against the wall as she reached the foot of the stairs. There was soft music playing. She reached the corner, paused for a heartbeat, then three. Finally, she poked her head out and saw four or five couples cuddling on some old couches draped with bedspreads. She hesitated. If she hadn't seen the vampire girl leading Jean-Pierre into the basement, this would be her cue to mutter, "Sorry," and tiptoe back upstairs. But she knew that something funky was going on. Something unnatural. Evil.

Then she heard the whimpering.

And the slurping.

Buffy turned on her flashlight and held it high above her head.

Five vampires, five human victims pinned beneath them. The vamps raised their faces and hissed at her. One of them was the fang-boy who had offered her a truce. Blood glittered on his lips.

"We meet again, Obi-Wan," Buffy said to him, reaching into her Slayer's bag. She brought out a cross and a stake. "Let's rumble."

"Get her!" the lying vampire shouted, and they moved toward her as one, a wall of living darkness.

Upstairs, the door slammed.

CHAPTER 3

Willow glanced at the door to the Bronze's basement. Buffy had gone down there after some vamp tramp several minutes earlier, and hadn't reappeared. "Maybe we should go after her," she suggested.

Xander pressed his lips together as he considered it. He raised his eyebrows. "She did tell us to stay here," he said. "You know how cranky Buffy gets when we ignore the Slayer's apprentice guidelines."

"She just worries about us, Xander," Willow said. "Buffy's all suped up with Slayer superpowers or something. We're just normal."

"Bite your tongue!" Xander scolded.

"Whatever," Willow said. "You know what I mean. Sometimes we can help, sometimes we're a handicap. Vampires don't spot you points for having your friends along. How many times did Superman almost die because he had Jimmy and Lois to worry about?"

"Wait, am I Lois or am I Jimmy?" Xander asked. Willow glared at him.

"All right," Xander surrendered. "I get it. But is this one of the times we can help or one of the times we'd be cramping her style?"

They looked at each other, then turned and stared at the door.

"That's the big question," Willow admitted.

Silence reigned for a sprinkling of seconds. Outside, the wind had suddenly died down. They glanced at each other again, and Willow opened her mouth to say something, but changed her mind.

"What?" Xander asked.

"Nothing."

"Something. What?" Xander prodded. "Come on."

"I think we should go after her," Willow suggested. "She could be in real trouble. If we don't look out for her, nobody else will. They all think she's psycho anyway."

"Right," Xander grumbled as he pushed off from his stool and headed for the basement door with Willow in tow.

A second later their path was blocked. Willow thought the blond guy in the cowboy getup was a total honey. He had these sideburns which were very out of date, but made him look steamy anyway. His eyes were a cold blue like nothing Willow had ever seen.

"Want to dance?" he asked, and Willow had to look around to make sure he was talking to her.

She grinned. So wide it hurt. Willow was about to say "Why not?" when she caught sight of the girl next to the smoking blond guy. She was dressed Old West trampy, a saloon girl to go along with Blue Eyes's cowboy outfit. Long red hair usually only found on TV. Eyes like chocolate. Eyes only for Xander. Willow liked Xander; Willow did not like the way this girl was looking at Xander, or the way Xander was looking back. For a moment, Blue Eyes was forgotten, as Willow tried to think of something witty to say to distract Xander from this girl.

The girl was wearing patent leather pumps, which were *way* over. Too dramatically unhip even for someone as I-don't-care-about-hip as Willow. Guy with sideburns. Girl with patent leathers.

"Xander," Willow said, and whacked him on the arm.

"Yeah," he answered, but didn't look away from the redhead.

"Xander," she said again. "I think this pair is a little too old for us."

"What?" he asked, turning to stare at her as if she were a psychonaut, somewhere in mental space.

Willow grabbed his arm, stood on tiptoe to whisper in his ear. "They're dead, you moron."

As Xander and Willow turned to examine the pair who'd started to hit on them, the two vampires grinned widely. Willow was sort of proud of herself, and relieved, at the same time that she was pretty wigged out. Maybe Buffy's undead radar was starting to rub off, or at least some of her fashion sense.

"Well?" said Blue Eyes, staring at Willow as if she were filet mignon. "Do you want to dance, or not?"

"That'd be option number two: not."

"Yeah, clone that for me," Xander agreed. "Sorry."

Xander and Willow began to move away, but almost as soon as they turned, the vampires slid up next to them. Blue Eyes grabbed Willow's arm tight enough to cut off circulation, and she could see that Red had done the same for Xander.

"We're all leaving now," Blue Eyes whispered to her. "Together. Out the front door. Scream, and we'll kill you here and now."

"Or later," Willow suggested nervously. "Later would be a big improvement on that idea. We could meet back here in, say, an hour, and you can exhibit your homicidal tendencies then, okay? That would be way better for us."

"Shutting up would be better for you," Red hissed at her as she strong-armed Xander toward the door.

"Okay, extreme time out here," Xander said loudly, drawing attention.

Red spun him around and practically spat in his face. "Another word and you're dead. We do not bluff."

"Okay," he muttered. "I can totally see that, but

you two are making such a ginormous goof here, and I thought I'd help you out before you ended up on the end of a stake."

"Mistake," Willow agreed, hoping Xander knew what he was doing. "Huge. Fatal. Hope your insurance is all paid up."

Blue Eyes held her wrist so tight Willow gritted her teeth waiting to hear the snapping of bones. It didn't happen. Oh, joy. All her limbs would remain intact until Blue Eyes sucked her dry.

"What are you two bloodbags talking about?" Blue Eyes demanded.

"Well," Xander said, still quietly, not wanting to rush headlong toward death, apparently. "See, it's like this. You both seem like nice bloodsucking fiends, and you," he indicated Red, "are better looking than any girl who's ever even spoken to me."

Red actually looked pleased.

"But, sad to say, we're with the Slayer," Xander went on. "And she's forbidden us to hang with you guys."

Blue Eyes and Red looked as if they'd each been slapped.

"The Slayer?" Red whispered.

"That's right," Xander continued. "So, y'know, I don't think you want to get all fang-ugly on us, right? Maybe if you scurry off right now, the Chosen One will spare your nasty selves until tomorrow night."

Blue Eyes and Red stared at them for several seconds, then exchanged an anxious glance.

"You have not seen the last of us," Blue Eyes

vowed, before the pair of vampires drifted off into the masquerade crowd.

"Promises, promises," Xander said, sighing.

"You behave now," Willow called after them. "Don't bite anyone I wouldn't bite."

She stood beside Xander and watched until the two Old West–costumed vampires were lost from sight.

"Well," Xander said, "that was interesting."

"Quite," Willow replied. "Good job, Xander." She wiped her forehead. She didn't know about Xander, but she'd been really sweating. "Maybe we should wait for Buffy after all?"

"Waiting." Xander nodded eagerly. "Original concept. Tremendous idea."

In the basement of the Bronze, Buffy stood her ground as five vampires—three guys and two girls—got up off the costumed teenagers they'd been using as unwilling blood donors. She glanced over at the victims and was relieved to see that, though either unconscious or way disoriented, they all seemed to be breathing.

Thank God for small respiratory favors.

"You've come at a bad time, Slayer," hissed the vampire with whom she'd agreed to a truce not half an hour before.

"I know, I know, you would've baked a cake. Well, I'm way sorry to interrupt the suckfest," Buffy sneered, "but haven't you leeches ever heard of the Red Cross?"

"Cold, lifeless blood," one of the vamp chicks growled. "We do not ask for our food, the warmth and life, we *take* it!"

"Take it?" Buffy chuckled. "You couldn't take a hint, never mind get a clue or buy a vowel."

The female vampire's face morphed into the typical extreme ugliness of her kind—like a Klingon burn victim with fangs. She roared and launched herself across the basement at Buffy. The Slayer waved her thick cross in front of her, and the other four vamps stayed back. Still, the first continued to rush forward.

"I don't believe in your God, Slayer!" the thing roared.

Buffy had the stake in her left hand and the cross in her right. When the vampire was almost on her, she ducked under its outstretched arms and slammed a hard uppercut to its gut, not bothering to use the stake for the moment. The vampire was stopped short, bent slightly, and Buffy brought her boot up into its face, knocking it over on its back. She straddled the fang-girl and sat down on her chest, all the time keeping the four other vamps in her peripheral vision. They were afraid of something—her or the cross, it didn't matter. Keeping them back was the key.

"Doesn't matter if you believe in God," Buffy said grimly, as the groggy vampire began to struggle to rise. "He believes in you."

She slammed the cross down on the vampire's face, and it burst into flame. Two of the other vamps shrieked. Buffy staked the fang-girl in the heart, and she exploded into blood-scented ashes.

"Better get the dustpan," she muttered as she stood and stared at the other four.

"Slayer," the liar began, glancing nervously at the crucifix in her hand, "perhaps we could discuss a truce again."

"Yeah, y'know, we could talk about that," Buffy began reasonably. "We could, maybe, have peace negotiations and . . . well . . . why not?"

The vampires stared at her.

"Really?" the liar asked.

"No." Buffy smiled. "Not really."

The liar began to growl, majorly pissed off at Buffy's mockery of him. The others began to creep forward, eyes on the cross.

"Oh, I'm so sorry," Buffy said innocently. "If this thing is giving you guys a wiggins, I'll just put it aside until we're through."

To the obvious astonishment of the undead, Buffy threw the cross on the cement about halfway between them. It clattered to the ground and stayed there.

"Now, unless you guys have some major elsewhere to be, why don't we fast forward to the juicy bits so I can return to my loitering amongst the tragically hip?" Buffy asked, switching the stake to her right hand.

A smile spread across the liar's face.

"Destroy her!" he shouted.

The four vamps rushed her together. Buffy

crouched and then launched herself high in the air—
higher than a normal teenage girl would have been
able to jump, but then, as Buffy often said, normal
was overrated. She grabbed hold of the thick copper
cold-water pipe running across the ceiling of the
basement, swung her legs, and tucked her head into
a somersault. She spun in the air and landed on her
feet, facing the backs of the four vampires.

They turned quickly to face her, but she'd thrown
off the focus of their attack. Buffy leaped again, into
a high roundhouse kick that nearly snapped the neck
of a fang-boy. He spun into another vampire and
Buffy went after them. She grabbed the vamp she'd
kicked around the neck, choking him, and used him
as a shield as she rammed the stake into the other's
chest. Even as the vamp disintegrated, she staked the
creature she'd kicked, and it disintegrated too.

"No more shield, no more games," the liar on her
right sneered, and Buffy spun to face him. The only
other surviving vampire, a fang-girl, was behind her
now, but she could almost sense the undead thing's
presence. Maybe her vampire radar was actually
starting to work? Or it could just have been the glare
from the vamp chick's screamingly tacky fashion
sense.

"Maybe this is, like, Scrabble for you," Buffy
snapped, "to me it's more like pest control."

"Vermin," the liar snarled.

"That is so my point," Buffy replied . . .

. . . then backed up a step and used both hands to
plunge the stake under her left armpit. Right into the

fang-girl who'd been about to rip her throat out from behind.

"Liar, liar," Buffy chided, and brought the stake in front of her again.

She was gaining a reputation as the Slayer. The creatures of darkness were wary of her. Buffy knew it would help her, give her an edge, to have them fear her. But she couldn't afford to get all celebrity-arrogant about it. There were no paparazzi for Slayers. If she let it go to her head, she'd be over, a bigger punchline than Dennis Rodman. She'd be dead.

The liar might be nervous around her, but that didn't mean he wasn't deadly.

They circled each other, as if they were acting out that fine drama known as professional wrestling. The liar ran his tongue across his bloodstained fangs.

"Y'know, they've got this way cool new invention called Crest," Buffy taunted him. "Give it a try. I'll bet you'd have a killer smile."

"That is the last time you'll mock me, Slayer," the liar declared.

"For once, you're right," Buffy agreed.

The liar lashed out at her. Buffy blocked with her left arm and slashed the tip of the stake across the vampire's face. The spilling of his own blood seemed to madden the creature, and he thundered toward her. The liar was too large, too powerful, for her to escape his grasp. He wrapped his arms around her and squeezed the breath out of her. Buffy knew her ribs were on the endangered list. She still had the stake, but couldn't get at his heart from the front and couldn't reach it from the back. A stab at the head or shoulder might distract him . . .

She slammed the stake into the back of the vampire's neck. He howled in pain and dropped her. Buffy scrambled back, picking up the fallen stake, and rose to her feet just as the furious vampire came after her again. There was no reason in its eyes now, only bloodlust and rage. It came after her.

Buffy ran.

But she didn't run far. Four long strides took her to the basement wall. The liar was breathing clammy air at her back, reaching for her. She didn't even slow as she leaped up, planted her feet on the wall, and did a backflip over him. The liar slammed into the wall, hard. She heard things cracking inside him.

When he turned to pursue her, Buffy staked him right through the heart.

On her way out of the basement, she picked up the cross and returned it to her bag along with the stake. The five victims in the corner were still alive, still breathing. She had checked to see that none of them had lost too much blood. Soon, they'd wake up in an extremely bad temper, probably assuming somebody had added a nasty something to their drinks.

At the top of the stairs, Buffy glanced over her shoulder into the darkness. Her heart had already slowed, but she still felt wound up, energized.

"Beats Jazzercise by a mile," she muttered to herself.

Then she rejoined the party.

Giles stared out one of the library windows at the neighborhood that surrounded Sunnydale High School. He'd been working all afternoon and into the evening and still hadn't come up with anything to substantiate his anxiety. Ever since Willow and Xander had told Buffy of the local legend concerning scarecrows and Halloween rain, he had been bothered by a feeling that he had read something similar somewhere. Some connection between Samhain, the spirit of Halloween, and scarecrows.

Every half hour or so, he would get up from his musty books and wander to the window. It had rained all day and through the early evening. Finally, the rain had begun to taper off. It was almost stopped now, but the hour had grown too late for children whose parents had kept them home due to the weather to set off on their Halloween candy-scavenging journey.

Still, there had been quite a number of children whose parents had not kept them home. Giles had seen them moving along out on the street and the side roads, in soaked costumes or with umbrellas, and he had come to a shocking realization. The neighborhood had followed through, no matter that it was unintentional, on the observance of Samhuinn, honoring the creatures of darkness. The rituals may have changed, but the offerings, the respect for supernatural power and the land of the dead, those had remained.

Samhain still had power.

Which bothered Giles quite a bit. There had been very little slaying for Buffy to do the past few weeks. He prayed she would not let her guard down because of this false sense of safety. It might prove a fatal error.

Now he walked back across the library. He imagined that he was probably the only person who would dare spend time in the place alone. It had been dark enough before he had begun to bring in his private collection. But with the evil bound within the volumes on the school library's shelves, the books themselves seemed to absorb any additional light that was brought into the room.

Giles sat down in a hard wooden chair and closed the book he'd been glancing through before taking a break. He scanned the table, noting which volumes he'd looked through already. At the far edge of the study table, a stack of thin volumes caught his eye: they were Watchers' Journals. He kept his own Watcher's Journal, a record of Buffy's exploits. But these were the chronicles of past Slayers.

"Hmm," he muttered to himself. "Perhaps."

Giles slid the tower of journals toward him, lifted the first from the stack, and began to read.

"Well, that was refreshing," Buffy said as she joined Willow and Xander in loitering orbit around the coffee bar. "I don't even need a caffeine fix."

"Buffy. Caffeine. Putting the fire out with gasoline," Xander mused. "Certain things are just so not a good idea."

"I assume that means we don't have any more sharp-toothed trouble to look forward to?" Willow asked.

Buffy smiled, glanced around the Bronze, and noticed at least half a dozen others who were probably vampires. Still, as long as she could keep an eye on them and they weren't misbehaving, she was determined to enjoy herself. The Slayer had been called upon to do her duty, and she had done it. The other vampires appeared not to know what had gone on downstairs, or else they didn't care that five of their kind had been destroyed. After all, they were not the most warm-hearted bunch.

"I'm glad you told me the assistant manager shut the basement door. Otherwise I might assume there was some kind of major plot to dust me. I think we'll be okay now," Buffy replied hopefully.

Apparently sensing Buffy's uncertainty, Willow sighed and raised her eyebrows.

"You must be a little rusty, huh?" she asked, changing the subject. "I mean, what with things having been so quiet until now. I assume the French kid, Jean-Pierre, is still alive."

"He'll be pretty light-headed from loss of blood, but he'll live," Buffy replied. "So will the others. And actually, I didn't feel rusty at all. Just . . . pumped."

"Pumped," Xander repeated, then shook his head in disbelief.

"Others?" Willow asked. "How many people were down there?"

"Five people, five vampires," Buffy replied. "Kind of like the buddy system, you know? Everybody pick a partner with fangs."

"Five?" Xander said, disturbed. "Next time, we are definitely part of the fangface posse."

"It was fine," Buffy insisted. "I was fine." It was true, too.

"Okay, whatever you say." Xander's eyes widened. "But how about wearing my jacket? You've got, like, blood, all over your blouse. Red is very in now, or so my many fashion-conscious friends tell me, but I think it clashes with the pirate queen motif . . . or goes too well. Just wear this."

As Xander slid his jacket off, Buffy glanced down at the blood on her blouse and made a totally grossed-out face. She thanked Xander distractedly as she put the jacket on.

"Much better," Willow said.

Now, it was time to start researching what kind of strategies were necessary to have a social life.

Buffy bobbed to the music of the Children of the Night, practically humming along even though she didn't understand a word. The singer mumbled about as badly as Astro on *The Jetsons*, only the real Astro—how virtual, a cartoon dog was more real— seemed to have an easier time getting his point across. Major Halloween grunge points for wearing costumes and for effort, but the band was five years too late and too musically challenged to be anything but a Seattle-schooled garage and cover band.

Sad commentary. They were the best band Buffy had seen at the Bronze. Then again, it was Sunnydale, after all. Boca del Infierno. If there was a rock n' roll heaven, they'd have a hell of a band. But rock n' roll hell was listening to mediocre covers of mediocre music, and that's what you got here in the Bad Place.

Still, Buffy was up. So up, the quality of the music was about three thousand miles from the point. The drought was over, it was raining vampires, hallelujah! She would gladly have swayed to Motorhead, if that was all she could get by way of tunes.

Xander and Willow gossiped, and Buffy chimed in when she had something particularly juicy to add or if she wanted more details. Gossip without the gory details was like black-and-white horror movies, all bark and no bite.

Chapter 4

Xander had zeroed in on a hotty none of them knew—but to whom Buffy had given a yes-this-chick's-alive stamp of approval—and moved in to ask for a dance. Or the somebody's-dad-had-too-much-to-drink-Hustle that passed for dancing where Xander was concerned.

To Buffy and Willow's severe non-surprise, the girl had blown him off.

"I just don't get women," Xander sighed as he pulled up a stool.

Buffy and Willow glared at him.

"Not you guys," he backpedaled. "I mean, you're not, like, *women* women. You're my buds, not catty females who . . . you're not into that girlie stuff, that . . . You two are the ultimate women of the millennium. Feminist ideal. Women. Great. Men.

Root of all evil. Cordelia, shallow witch. Buffy and Willow . . . not."

Xander swallowed, eyes wide, and glanced at Buffy and Willow hopefully. "Just didn't want you guys—uh, girls, to get the wrong idea."

"Wrong idea," Buffy repeated, eyebrows raised. "Of course not."

She glanced at Willow, nodded, and they each reached out and grabbed hold of one of Xander's ears.

"Oowwwww!" he howled.

"That was an almost-save, Xander," Willow told him. "But almost only counts in—"

"Horseshoes and hand grenades," Xander finished. "I know, I know, now let go, okay? You know I love you guys."

The girls let go and Xander rubbed his ears, felt them, possibly trying to be certain they were still attached.

"Well, Buffy," Willow said. "You've saved Halloween, right? And the vampires who hit on Xander and me have Jimmy Hoffa'd, so maybe we can actually hang out and enjoy the rest of the masquerade."

"Aye-aye to that," pirate queen Buffy agreed. "I've had my share of Halloween tricks."

"It is so time for the treats," Xander said.

"Let's find some chocolate," Willow added eagerly.

Buffy laughed. They began to move toward the snack bar when the door slammed open and Mr. O'Leary blew into the Bronze.

Glenn O'Leary was the town psycho. Well, besides Buffy, of course. But he'd been at it much longer than she had, and had greater celebrity because it wasn't just the high school kids who thought he was a few fries short of a Happy Meal. The whole town thought he was damaged merchandise.

Inside the Bronze, raving like a street-corner preacher with a heavy Irish accent, he was very convincing as a nut job.

"They've come back for us!" Mr. O'Leary shouted. "The dead are risin' from their graves, diggin' out from the earth, wet with Halloween rain. They're comin' for us all!"

"So much for treats," Buffy said miserably.

Long, heavy sigh.

As the band thrashed on, the strange man dropped his hands to his sides and looked defeated. "They're risin', sure as I'm an O'Leary," he insisted, looking bewildered as the kids lost interest and drifted away.

He approached the next person who came near him, who wasn't a person at all but a vampire, and took his arm. The vampire, whose costume was apparently the leather jacket and hair gel that made him look like John Travolta in *Grease,* stopped and regarded Mr. O'Leary with amusement.

"What's that you say, Grandpa?" the vampire asked, egging the old man on.

"Risin'! The dead risin' up out o' their graves!"

"You haven't lived around here very long, have you?" the vampire asked, taunting the old man.

Fang-boy looked around and preened as some nearby partyers chuckled and applauded. He actually looked like a normal, sarcastic American guy for a second or two. Hmm, maybe it was a simple self-esteem problem that compelled them to murder human beings. With some positive reinforcement, perhaps they could be made useful members of society. Like Cordelia.

"Don't mock me, me boyo," the old man said. "I barely escaped with me life to come and warn you! I've lived here in Sunnydale for near twenty years."

"Then you should know that around here the dead are always rising from their graves," the vampire sneered. "It's dead folks that put Sunnydale on the map."

"I told you not to mock me!" Mr. O'Leary cried. "I seen it meself, with me own two eyes! Clawin' and crawlin' up out o' their graves, shamblin' around the cemetery in search o' somethin', and I don't want to know what it is!"

The vampire brushed Mr. O'Leary off and wandered away. The rest of the masqueraders just did their best to uncomfortably ignore the crazy old man. Buffy was sad for Glenn O'Leary. They were kind of kindred spirits. Sunnydale did its best to ignore her the same way they did him—ignore her, and the evils that she saved their bacon from almost every night.

"I so don't want to even bring this up," Buffy said, "but have you guys considered the majorly-depressing possibility that the old guy isn't as follow-my-nose Fruit Loopy as the rest of the town has an aching desire to believe?"

Willow and Xander exchanged a glance, looked at Buffy, then back at each other.

"Xander, know what I truly hate?" Willow asked.

"In fact, yes," Xander said. He took a deep breath, and they turned back to look at Buffy again. "You hate when Buffy's right," he said. "Which I know, because I'm right there with you. Hate that. Totally."

"Because when Buffy's right it usually means blood, death, maybe some recreational flesh-eating," Willow said, and raised an eyebrow as she stared at Buffy.

"Fine!" Buffy sniffed. "If you guys want, I could just leave you in the dark on all this. Next time there's some demonic force or serial-killing ape monster on the loose, you'll be off the James Bond, eyes-only, need-to-know list. Aren't you thrilled!"

"Not so fast," Xander said nervously. "Darkness not good. Nobody said anything about—y'know, we're the Slayerettes, right?"

"You're our beacon of light in the darkness," Willow said, wide eyed and with as much sincerity as she could manufacture on a moment's notice. "And you're right, of course. The rest of the town is psycho. Nobody sees anything, or will talk about it. They all want to pretend Sunnydale is as sunny as Sunnybrook Farm."

"Which is where?" Xander asked, looking at Willow strangely.

"In a book," Buffy replied, shaking her head. "Where you might think about sticking your nose once in a while."

"You've never read *Rebecca of Sunnybrook Farm?*" Willow asked, horrified.

"Sounds like a girl book," Xander said, then fumbled, "about a girl. A book about a girl. Named Rebecca."

"Anyway, you're right about the major denial that's happening here," Willow went on. "Doesn't it strike you as odd that with all the strangeness that goes on, we don't rate a Scully-and-Mulder moment or two?"

"Will, I hate to break it to you," Buffy said with a little wink, "but those guys are just pretend."

Willow gave her head a shake. "You know what I mean. Giles always has me looking online through the newspapers for information about the Hell-mouth. The stories are all there—gruesome deaths, missing persons reports, maximum weirdness all over the place—but nobody connects the dots."

"Because nobody wants to," Buffy said, understanding. Xander and Willow nodded. She looked again at the raving Irishman. "Maybe it's time for the Slayer to have a chat with Mr. O'Leary."

"They're comin' out o' the ground!" the old man shouted.

"Hey, Mr. O'Leary," said an older man, maybe about thirty-five or forty, wearing nicely pressed jeans, a Grateful Dead T-shirt, and a ponytail. He firmly took Mr. O'Leary by the arm and steered him toward the coffee bar. "Why don't you sit down and I'll make you a nice cup of Irish coffee."

Willow gestured at the man in the T-shirt. "That's Nick Daniels. He's the assistant manager of the Bronze." She lowered her voice. "He was a student of Mr. O'Leary's a long time ago. A lot of people in this room were his students." She sighed. "He was fired about ten years ago."

"Coffee!" Mr. O'Leary cried. "Isn't anyone listening to me?"

Buffy murmured, "I am," and looked at her two pals. "Looks like I'm on duty again." She slid off her chair. "Watch my bag for me, okay?"

Xander looked excited. "Okay," he said. "And can we rummage through it?"

Buffy shrugged. "Sure, Xander. It's not as if I'll lose my membership in the secret society of vampire Slayers if mere mortals take a gander at the tools of the trade." She gave him a half-hearted smile, envying his status as a perpetual spectator. "Enjoy."

As Buffy turned to go, she heard Xander say to Willow, "Poor woman. No wonder she's not dating. Can you imagine her getting to sit through an entire movie?"

"So you wouldn't want to go to the movies with Buffy?" Willow asked.

"You kidding?" he said quickly. "I'd sit through the Meg Ryan chick flick marathon with Buffy."

As she walked off, Buffy heard Willow sigh, and she wanted to smack Xander. Willow and Xander went together like Shaggy and Scooby, vampires and stakes, studying and passing. Why couldn't that blind guy see it?

". . . zombies," Mr. O'Leary was saying to Nick Daniels, as the assistant manager sprayed whipped cream on top of a cup of coffee. Daniels picked up a chocolate shaker and looked questioningly at Mr. O'Leary. "Are you daft, man? What do I care for sugar sprinkles and cream at a time like this?"

"Mr. O'Leary?" Buffy began, coming up behind him.

Mr. O'Leary swiveled on his stool and looked at her. Looked again, harder. His lips parted.

Something passed between them, some strange connection like a very mild electric current. He seemed to feel it, too, for he pulled away from her slightly. Without looking away from her, he picked up his coffee cup and took a sip. His hand shook.

"Who are you?" he asked slowly.

"My name is Buffy," she began. "Buffy Summers. I was, ah, curious about what you were saying." Nick Daniels leaned on the counter, clearly without plans to move along and do some other assistant-manager type of thing. "About the graveyard."

He took another sip of coffee and turned his gaze toward Daniels. "Nick, boy," he said kindly, "would you be making my friend Buffy Summers here a drink with that fancy machine o' yours?"

Daniels looked at Buffy. "May I have a latte?" she asked, quickly adding, "Decaf? Nonfat milk?"

"Sure." Daniels looked concerned, as if by going to use the espresso machine, he would leave her vulnerable and helpless. If only he knew. But go he did, and Buffy inwardly sighed with relief.

"Now," Buffy said, climbing up on the stool

beside Mr. O'Leary. She folded her hands and put them on the bar. "Please. Tell me."

"And why would you be wanting to know, miss?" Mr. O'Leary asked carefully.

She shrugged. "I'm a curious sort of girl."

"Oiy, that y'are," he replied. "But of what sort, I'm uncertain."

His accent reminded her of Michael J. Fox in *Back to the Future III* when he played his own Irish immigrant great-grandfather. Sometimes it concerned her that her head was filled with so many pop-culture references that she had one for every occasion. Maybe the reason she wasn't doing too hot in school was because she didn't have room in her brains for any more stuff. Or it could be all the gory extracurriculars.

"Give me dish," she urged. "I mean, please tell me what you saw."

He stared downward and whispered something. She leaned in. *Now* he mumbled.

"The dead are risin'. They are coming up from their graves to destroy the living."

"Um, could you be more specific?" she asked. "That covers an awful lot of territory."

He frowned. "Who *are* you?"

"Someone who believes you," she said softly. "Mr. O'Leary, these dead people. What kind of dead people are they?"

He looked as if he might cry. "Do you know how long I've been thought insane? My teaching job—" He swallowed hard. "Everything lost. But it's all true."

Buffy covered his hand. "I know, Mr. O'Leary."

They looked at each other without speaking. A single tear ran down his cheek.

"My country's folk tales speak of heroes. This place is in desperate need of one."

"I know that, too." She gave his hand a little squeeze. "Please, Mr. O'Leary, tell me before Mr. Daniels comes back with my coffee."

"Zombies, they are," he said in a rush. "Do you know of Samhuinn?"

"Yes, a little." She wished she'd paid better attention to Giles's lecture. It occurred to her that she often wished that. She just wasn't used to doing the listening thing.

"The dark time of year, when the pumpkin king reigns."

"The pumpkin king?" Confused, she scratched her cheek. "I'm not tracking. What about the zombies?"

"He holds dominion over all." Mr. O'Leary's voice began to rise. "Creatures awaken to do his bidding. Werewolves. Zombies. Demons. They strike like warriors to thin our ranks while he searches for the one."

Buffy was silent while she processed that. Then she said, "The one."

She blinked. Uh-oh. "Would that one be called a, um, Slayer?"

He looked at her blankly. "That's a name I've not heard."

"Oh." She brightened slightly. "Good. I mean, oh, how interesting."

"Interesting?" He stared at her for a moment just as Mr. Daniels put her mug on the bar. Then Mr. O'Leary threw his coffee cup to the floor. It smashed and coffee and whipped cream flew everywhere. "You're just as thick as the rest of 'em! I didn't come here to tell stories. I came for help against the forces of evil."

"What's going on here?" a woman's voice asked pleasantly. She was thirty-something, but barely showed it. She wore a totally hip navel-baring button-down shirt and cotton print pants. Her name badge read Claire Bellamy, Manager. Nick Daniels came out from around the bar and joined her.

"I thought you understood me," Mr. O'Leary shouted, pointing at Buffy. "That you were going to do something!"

Daniels and Bellamy looked at Buffy. Though she felt bad doing it, she moved her shoulders and said, "I don't know what he's talking about."

"You, you—" Mr. O'Leary sputtered. Then, at the top of his lungs, he bellowed, "You little liar!"

Heads turned. Buffy cleared her throat, trying to hint that they would get more accomplished if he'd be a little sly about it.

"Okay, Mr. O'Leary," Claire Bellamy said. "I'm going to have to ask you to leave. Nick, a hand?"

Mr. O'Leary raised a finger at Buffy as the manager and assistant manager shuffled him firmly toward the exit. "If more die, it's on your head, Buffy Summers!"

"Could you say that into the P.A. system, please?" Buffy said under her breath. "There may be a few people who didn't hear that." Not to mention a vampire or two.

From their perches, Xander and Willow made oh, great expressions. Buffy pointed to herself and then to the door. The two jumped down and joined her. Xander said, "Buffy Summers, you little liar person, what are you going to do now?"

"Well, I don't suppose I'm going to Disney World," Buffy said glumly. "I guess I'm going to the graveyard."

She reached out her hand for her Slayer's bag, which Xander was carrying. He had her box of matches in his hand and she knew he was dying to ask her what she used them for. If she told him they were for just in case, like to light a candle, she knew he would be disappointed.

At that moment, thunder shook the Bronze. The lights flicked off and the band wound down like a tired battery-operated toy. The only light in the place was from the candles in the grinning pumpkins on the tables. The faces above them—both human and vampire—looked eerie and skeletal.

"Wow, cool," Xander said. He cleared his throat. "I mean, oh, what a drag."

The lights flicked back on. Everybody cheered.

Buffy looked down at her elbow and said, "Anybody want a nonfat decaf latte?"

"This time we're going with you," Willow insisted.

Xander nodded. "We don't want you to get your brains eaten by zombies."

Willow added, "You might be outnumbered. I

mean, really outnumbered, if there are, like, a kabil-lion of them and only one of you."

"I'm the Slayer, guys."

"These are zombies, not horrible demons or ultra-strong vampires," Willow said reasonably. "I think civilians are allowed to kill them, like a citizen's arrest, y'know." She looked a little nervous. "I mean, don't they just stumble around real slow?"

"Stumbling's what I've heard," Xander agreed. "They do that sort of mummy-stumble thing." He puffed out his chest. "Most definitely can I run faster than a speeding zombie. Hey, I won third place for the fifty-yard dash at camp the summer before sixth grade."

Willow smiled patiently at him, then turned to Buffy. "There, you see? Proof positive of our suit-ability for the mission."

Buffy wasn't convinced. She said, "If Giles says it's okay, you can come." Figuring that he'd most likely say no, especially once she told him the bit about the dark lord. "I need to call him anyway and see if he has any fun facts and helpful tips on how to deal with zombies that I didn't get from watching *Dawn of the Dead*."

Xander shuddered. "I loved that movie the first time I saw it. I never dreamed I'd be in one of the sequels."

Buffy smiled ironically. "Stick with me, baby. I'll make you a star." She pointed to the door that led to the bathrooms and the Bronze's two phones. The phones were always being used, usually by people making up or breaking up. Cellular had not hit Sunnydale in a big way, at least not among the kids. In L.A., everyone had pagers. She just hoped there wasn't much of a line for the lines of communication.

Special Agents Harris and Rosenberg flanked Buffy as they worked their way through the Bronze. Then Buffy pushed open the door just as a zombie stumbled out.

She drew back her arm and was about to smash its face in when it said, "If you're going to use the phone, they're, like, out."

"What?" Buffy said. She ran to the phones and tried both of them as Xander and Willow looked on. "They don't work."

"I'll ask to use the Bronze's private line," Xander suggested and dashed off, leaving Willow and Buffy alone.

"Poor Mr. O'Leary," Willow said. "Nobody believes him."

"Clone that thought," Buffy said, thinking of the tears in Mr. O'Leary's eyes. She felt as if she had betrayed him. But what else could she have done? "I wonder if I'll end up like that, Willow. You know, Giles refuses to tell me the average Slayer life span. You notice how it's always one *girl* in every generation? Not one middle-aged matron in every generation? One bridge-playing—"

"—Harley-riding," Willow threw in.

Buffy blinked. "I don't own a Harley."

"You don't play bridge, either."

Xander poked his head in. "Their phone's out, too. Word on the street is that the lines went down in the storm. And I could not find one living soul who had a cell phone." He shrugged. "I didn't ask the dead ones."

"Oh, well," Willow said unhappily.

"Oh, well, nothing," Buffy shot back. "I want you two to go to Giles and see if he can dig anything up about zombies." She snapped her fingers. "Oh, yeah, and about the pumpkin king."

"Tim Burton flick. *Nightmare Before Christmas*," Xander supplied helpfully. "He wants to be Santa Claus."

Buffy looked at Willow. Willow said, "I'll ask him about the pumpkin king."

"And the dark lord, too," Buffy said, wrinkling her nose. There were too many big-shot bad guys interrupting her good times.

"I'm not certain I'm liking this split-up maneuver," Xander said. "In the movies, the kids split up and then the dude with the chain saw shows up."

Buffy said, "Hmm." What she was thinking was, maybe the term dude wasn't so over after all. When she realized Xander thought she was reconsidering her insistence that he and Willow go to Giles, she shook her head. "Xander, I need his input."

"Let's all three go, then," Xander said.

"I need to go now. Who knows what's going on over there? Besides, I'm worried about Mr. O'Leary. He might try to save the world all by himself."

"Saving the world all by oneself. Sound like anyone we know, Agent Rosenberg?" Xander said in his best David Duchovny voice.

"Indeed, Agent Harris," Willow replied. "But as much as I hate to admit it, Buffy has a point. I'm thinking we should be obedient little Slayerettes."

Xander scrunched up his face. "That's your thought?"

"Yes. The thought that I have," Willow said.

"Okay." Buffy clapped her hands. "Synchronize your watches. Let's hit the streets."

"Jolly Roger, Captain." Xander saluted. Then he got serious and said, "Don't do anything I wouldn't do."

Buffy grinned. "Can't think of anything offhand, Xander, but okay."

The three of them hurried out of the Bronze and out into the Halloween night together. Buffy hoped they were more Three Musketeers than Three Stooges. If they were the Stooges, she didn't think Larry and Curly were going to survive the night.

CHAPTER 5

In the silence of the library, Giles sat and pored through the many volumes of Watchers' Journals. The exploits of the Slayers of the past made for some horrifying and exciting reading, but he had no time to be fascinated by any of it. As the night wore on, he found that instead of being relieved that he hadn't heard from Buffy, he became more and more concerned. He couldn't shake the feeling that something was going to happen, or was happening even now.

It had to do with Halloween, with Samhuinn, the season of the dead. And with that local legend about scarecrows and Halloween rain. Of that he was certain. But though he had been equally certain that he'd once read references to Samhain, the demonic spirit of Halloween, in connection with scarecrows, he hadn't yet come across any mention of either thing.

Disgusted and in a hurry, Giles had resorted to something he despised: skimming. Now his eyes whipped across journal pages and he looked for any references to the Druids, the Celts, scarecrows, Samhuinn, or Samhain.

Nothing. Or, as he'd heard Buffy say many times, "no joy."

Giles pushed up his glasses and rubbed his eyes. He was tired, but he hadn't begun to drift off yet. That was something, at least. He had to stay awake. Buffy's life might depend upon it.

On the other hand, and this was a thought he'd kept avoiding because his instincts screamed otherwise, it was possible that he was wrong. It was possible that any connection between local legends and ancient Halloween demons was just in his head, and Buffy wasn't in any real danger. That Sunnydale was not going to be overrun by the minions of the Halloween king.

Slowly, Giles became aware of a certain anxiety, a feeling of dread that had snuck up on him. He tried to pinpoint the source of this feeling, to identify it. Then he did. There was a warmth on his back, that feeling he'd always gotten when someone was staring at him. Watching him. Sizing him up, maybe for a next meal.

He turned, narrowing his eyes and peering at the doorway and the darkened hall beyond. Giles blinked twice, trying to focus, but there was nothing there to focus on. Nobody watching him. Watching the Watcher. A shiver ran through him, just a little excess energy he'd stored while concentrating so hard on his research. At least, that's what he was going to tell himself.

Rupert Giles was not a nervous person by nature, not anxiety prone or jumpy at all, in fact. He'd prided himself on that fact. It had served him well as a Watcher, and in all the years of study he'd had to prepare for that role. He was simply not easily spooked.

Somewhere in the school, down the hall a way, a door closed. Just short of a slam, it was, but loud enough for Giles to hear it. Giles glanced around at the door again.

Curiosity got the better of him and he rose from his chair and strode across the gloomy library to the door. He poked his head out into the hallway and looked in both directions. The hall was empty. If he'd been asked, he would have thought the school was empty. Now, however, it seemed as though he was not alone.

"Just the custodian," he assured himself, as he returned to his chair and began skimming journals again.

A sudden thought gave him pause. He'd been sure the custodian had already left for the evening.

Giles brushed the thought aside. He'd spent many a late night in the library without incident. In truth, while most people were deeply disturbed by being alone in a place that was usually populated—a school, or office, for example—Giles preferred it.

Easier to concentrate, he'd always felt. No jumping at shadows for him.

Suddenly, his eyes fell upon the word Samhain in the journal he'd been reading. He scanned back to the beginning of that entry, and began to read.

"Mr. Giles?"

"Aaah!" Giles cried out, and leaped to his feet, knocking the chair onto the floor with a *clack* as he spun to see who had spoken to him.

Wayne Jones, the white-haired custodian, stood in the doorway to the library with a broom in his hand, frowning at Giles's reaction.

"Ah, Mr. Jones," Giles said, trying to calm his pounding heart and cover his embarrassment. "You startled me."

"Sorry about that, Mr. Giles," the older man said in his gravelly voice. "I see you're burning the midnight oil as usual. I just wanted to tell you I was locking up, make sure you had your keys and see if there was anything you needed me to do in here before I go."

"Hmm? Oh, no, thank you," Giles said. "Have a good evening, Mr. Jones."

"You, too, Mr. Giles," Jones said. "Sorry again about frightening you."

"Frightening . . ." Giles said absently, rubbing the back of his neck, as he often did when he found a subject of conversation uncomfortable. "Not at all. I'm just a bit on edge, actually. You go on, I'll be all right."

"See you tomorrow," the custodian said as he started off down the hall again.

"Yes, yes," Giles said, turning back to the journal once more.

He'd found a reference to Samhain in the Watcher's Journal referring to the exploits of a Slayer named Erin Randall, an Irish girl who'd lived in the seventeenth century. The Watcher, Timothy Cassidy, had been very fond of the girl, and if Giles's memory served, Erin had been the Slayer for only a short time before her death. She'd died violently, as most Slayers did in the end. But in her short term as the Chosen One, she had faced a horde of demons, monsters, and vampires. Even the Tatzelwurm, which she had destroyed.

"I ought to have known it would be you," Giles whispered to himself. "Who else could have faced Samhain and lived?"

Giles paused then, upset by the question. Could Buffy battle Samhain and survive? It wasn't even certain that Samhain was here, in Sunnydale, but Giles suspected that if the spirit of Halloween, the demon king of ancient Druidic rituals, was going to settle anywhere, it would be the Hellmouth.

He pushed his concern away. Buffy had become quite accomplished as the Slayer in a very short time. What she lacked in her studies, she more than made up for through determination, physical skill, and sheer courage. If Buffy couldn't stop Samhain, Giles suspected the Halloween king couldn't be stopped. Somehow, the thought did little to comfort him.

"Ah, here we are," he muttered, as he found the journal entry and began to read.

The Randall lass is but a wee slip of a girl [the Watcher Cassidy had written], yet now she must face one of the most powerful demons born of the time before man. The Vikings and the French paid their respects to this demonic spirit, the lord of the night, whom the dead and the creatures of darkness all obey.

Let me amend my words to this: that they did obey him in the days of old. Through the lifting of the veils of superstition and ignorance, the dark lord, Samhain, has lost much of his power. 'Tis a good thing, for otherwise my young lady would not dare hope to defeat him.

Aye, once 'pon a time, the Celts, the ancient people of my own land, green Ireland, did hide away from Samhain and his followers for all the long winter months. That was the dead time, called Samhuinn, called thus after the old demon himself. Feasts there were, for the dead. Candles burned all of a night to keep the dead away, and offerings bought lives for another day. The folk carved pumpkins to represent the dread lord of the winter, and Samhain rejoiced. He reigned supreme as the pumpkin king, the spirit of the dead time.

The dark lord, some called him.

But power cannot stay forever, and the time of the Druid priests came to an end. Through the grace of God, the heathen Celts became Christian Irish, and the season of the dead began to wither like unto a tree denied life-saving water. Soon, Samhuinn was a three-day festival, a holiday, and the old faith was gone. Hallowe'en had taken its place.

The pumpkin king was enraged, but could do nothing. He would survive, of course. He had been there before the Celts, before humanity, and he would remain. But he was weakened. Samhain could enter the world only through a vessel built in his image. There must be a little faith, at the least, for him to return.

Jack-o'-lanterns, carved pumpkins, would serve him as hosts, even if their makers did not know they were following the ancient rituals. Jack-o'-lanterns are the eyes of Samhain, the eyes of the king of Hallowe'en. He can see everything that they see, but he cannot act, for he himself has no form.

There is only one form the old demon may use to walk the earth now. Many farmers, too foolish to realize what they have done, have provided Samhain with host bodies by making scarecrows for their fields and using carved pumpkins for the scarecrows' heads.

Last night, All Hallow's Eve, the dead walked the English countryside, the werewolves and ghouls, ghosts and goblins along with them. And they had their king to lead them. My lady the Slayer, Erin Randall, was kept busy through the night by various creatures of darkness, and she was forewarned by them that the pumpkin king had set his sights on her, that tonight he planned to take her life.

I have provided Erin with garlic and angelica for her protection, with signs and sigils which she may draw in the ground to trap the demon—a feat which may also be accomplished with a ring of fire—and I have given her a weapon of my own making which may, I pray, destroy the host vessel. Mayhap this will return Samhain to the netherworld, where he resides the rest of the year. Or perhaps it will destroy the pumpkin king forever.

Giles studied the markings on the page, the symbols and designs which, when drawn in a circle in the dirt, would apparently trap Samhain, as in a sacred circle. He memorized the parts used to make the ancient Slayer's weapon. Then he moved on, to read about Erin Randall's battle with Samhain. According to Cassidy's journal, Samhain had managed to disarm the girl, so the weapon was never used. She had, instead, found a way to destroy the scarecrow host body, thus banishing Samhain for another year. This part was a bit vague; Cassidy had been interrupted while writing and hadn't filled in all the blanks.

The pumpkin king must have been furious, Giles

thought, and wondered what had happened the next year. He flipped pages until he came to the following Halloween's entry. The last entry, as it turned out. For the following year, Samhain killed Erin Randall.

Giles closed the book, turned and stared at the moonlight shining through the library window.

"Buffy," he whispered to himself.

He stood quickly, picked up a canvas bag, and began to gather items he knew he would need. Then he hurried out of the library.

Xander and Willow were tired. They'd made good time, and the high school was definitely within walking distance, but it wasn't a short walk. All the while, they'd been glancing over their shoulders, expecting trouble to come leaping out at them at any moment. Despite what Buffy had hoped, Halloween night was turning out to be pretty horrible. Xander himself had hoped for some quality time with Buffy—and Willow too, of course. No such luck. At this point, he figured he'd have to be dead to spend any real time with the Slayin' babe of his dreams.

And as romantic as he'd always considered himself, that was really not an option.

He and Willow stepped onto the campus lawn and started across toward the front of the school. As they passed by the bench where they met every morning, there was a sudden snapping sound behind them, and they both turned and stared up into a nearby tree.

"Not good," Xander said.

"We're just jumpy, is all," Willow said, offering some of her famous rationalization. One of the reasons she had been Xander's best friend since kindergarten. "What with the night we're having, we'd have to be extreme morons not to be a little nervous."

"Right," Xander agreed. "A little nervous."

Somewhere off in the dark, they could hear a high, child-like laugh.

"Ignore it, Xander," Willow said. "Let's move."

They picked up their pace, heading for the front steps of the school.

"There's nothing to be afraid of," Willow insisted. "Right? I mean, what do we have to fear?"

Xander glared at her out of the corner of his eye, even as he walked faster.

"Oh, I don't know," he muttered. "How about zombies and werewolves and vamps?"

"Oh my," Willow gasped.

Xander rolled his eyes. "What is it with you and the *Wizard of Oz* references? Zombies and werewolves and vamps, oh my. Zombies and werewolves and—"

"Vamps," Willow finished, and whacked him in the chest.

Finally Xander realized that her Oh my hadn't been a film reference, but an actual gasp of oh-boy-we're-in-trouble-now astonishment. He followed her gaze and saw that they weren't alone. They really had been followed.

"Well, well, what have we here?" sneered the blond-haired fang-boy Willow had nicknamed Blue Eyes.

"Miss me, baby?" asked his sidekick, the vamp chick they'd dubbed Red, batting her long lashes at Xander.

"Like a hole in the head," Xander grumbled. "Or two in the neck. One hundred people surveyed, top five answers on the board. Number one answer is no. Definitely no."

The vampires began to move across the grass toward them.

"We've been following you," Blue Eyes growled. "The Slayer isn't around now to protect you. You're just another pair of bloodbags, just meat. Let's see if you're as brave without the Chosen One to protect you."

"Bravery is extremely overrated," Willow said. She reached out and gripped Xander's hand.

"Absolutely," Xander agreed nervously, as the vampires split apart, moving to trap him and Willow between them. "There are so many ways to respond to danger that are more constructive than bravery."

"Name one," Red sneered through perfect pouty lips that almost distracted Xander from the danger.

"Oh, I don't know," he mumbled. "Well, then, there's running!"

Dragging Willow along, Xander bolted for the school. A second later, she passed him and he let go of her hand. The vampires roared and ran in pursuit. The stairs were just ahead, but he knew they weren't going to make it.

"Willow!" he shouted. "Open the door!"

Xander reached behind his back, under the white shirttail that had been hanging down over his pants. He yanked a cross from his belt and stopped short, turned, and lifted the cross to face the vampires.

"Xander!" Willow cried in alarm behind him. Then he heard her begin to bang on the door, screaming for Giles.

Blue Eyes and Red hissed as they stumbled to a halt on the lawn. The vampires were taken off guard, but Xander knew that in a second they'd be moving in on him again like social-climbing sophomores after Cordelia. Holding the cross behind him, he stumbled toward the stairs.

"What in the world?" Giles's voice came from behind him, and Xander knew that was his cue.

Fast as he could manage, he loped up the stairs, pushing through the double doors past Willow and Giles. As they slammed the doors, Blue Eyes and Red were pounding up the steps. Giles and Willow hurried, but Red got a hand inside and reached her clawed fingers toward Willow's face. The doors were crushing her arm, but the vampire kept coming. Blue Eyes slammed against the door, trying to force it open.

"Denied!" Xander shouted, and slapped the cross down on Red's bare arm.

The vamp chick howled in agony and withdrew,

but in a heartbeat, Blue Eyes was there, propping open the door with his foot.

"Xander!" Willow shouted.

The cross was still gripped in his hand. Xander hurled it at Blue Eyes's forehead. It struck him there and he fell back as if the Hulk had popped him one, the flesh of his face smoking.

Willow and Giles were finally able to get the doors closed. Xander rammed the bolts on the top and bottom of the doors into their respective holes, then stood, breathing heavily, as the vampires began to slam against the doors from outside.

"Either I'm having a heart attack or Neve Campbell has agreed to be my bride," Xander huffed, and turned to face Willow and Giles, who stared at him grimly.

"Not that I'm not happy that you produced that cross from thin air," Willow said. "But have you been carrying that around all night?"

Xander looked away. "Not exactly. When I was riffling through Buffy's Slayer bag, I kind of borrowed it. I figured it might come in handy, and she had another one."

He shrugged.

"Well," Giles sniffed, "I, for one, am pleased with your sudden burst of kleptomania. Without it, we might be dead now."

"Thanks," Xander said. "I think."

"So what now?" Willow asked.

"We do seem to be in a bit of a pickle," Giles commented.

"Enough with the condiments," Xander began, but Giles interrupted.

"I'm sorry, Xander, but we've no time for the usual banter. It seems your story about pumpkin-headed scarecrows and Halloween rain may be true after all. I suspect that Samhain, the demon spirit who once ruled Halloween, may be out to destroy Buffy. Your appearance here tells me it hasn't been a quiet night."

"Only if you call vampires and zombies a quiet night," Willow said.

"Which may have been sent after Buffy by Samhain himself," Giles muttered, almost to himself. "We've got to get out of here. It seems our Slayer may have gotten herself into serious trouble."

"Maybe you haven't noticed, Giles," Xander replied. "But we're in a bit more than kinda sorta trouble ourselves, here. Any ideas how we're going to get to Buffy to warn her about the Halloween demon guy?"

Giles pushed his glasses up the bridge of his nose, raised his eyebrows, and smiled thinly. "Well," he said, "we're just going to have to slay those vampires outside, now aren't we?"

CHAPTER 6

When zombies rose, they scrabbled like rats as they clawed their way out of their graves. You'd almost think they were suffocating below the earth and needed the fresh air, the way they struggled.

At least, that was one Slayer's opinion as she sat on top of the locked wrought-iron entrance gates of the Sunnydale Cemetery. Gray hands coated with slime and crawling with earthworms shot out of the ground and searched for something, anything, to grab on to—a bush, a headstone, another zombie— to pull the rest of the zombie out.

Make that *most* of the rest of the zombie.

Sometimes things were left behind in the effort, like an arm or a leg or a face. But that didn't seem to matter as they got free of the grave and started doing their zombie thing.

Of all the forces of evil Buffy had to fight, zombies

were probably the grossest. No way was she delighted to go in there and mess with them.

But when zombies rose, they were hungry.

For human brains.

They would do just about anything for a bite or two.

The walking dead smelled dinner, and its name was Buffy.

They must have smelled the rest of Sunnydale, too, because about a dozen of them had clumped into a mosh pit at the stone wall, and they were pushing to get the heck out of the cemetery and cruise for munchies. The wall so far had not given way. But farther down, a second bunch was pushing on another section. Several small stones had chipped out of the cement grout and clattered to the sidewalk on the other side.

Beneath her perch atop the gates, fifteen or twenty shambling corpses, in different stages of decay, surged against the iron bars. The chain that held the gates closed screeched, as did the iron hinges. It wouldn't be long before one or the other gave way and the zombies would be out on the streets of Sunnydale.

Buffy tried not to look at them. The dead faces, some just bare skulls with tufts of skin and hair here and there, gaped up at her. There was a moaning coming from the dead that gave her a major wiggins, a shiver all through her. It was like putting her ear to a seashell, only much worse. She couldn't tell if it was their voices, or just the wind whistling through their exposed bones and skulls. That sound was worse than Cordelia's whining, and even more likely to drive her crazy.

"Okay, you guys have killer harmonies. En Vogue are sweating right now," she muttered. "But could you please *shut up!*"

The zombies didn't respond at all, just continued to moan and stare. Some of them were staring without eyes, and Buffy so did not want to know what they were seeing.

She glanced out over the cemetery as more zombies clawed out of their graves. There were an awful lot of them. Sunnydale seemed like such a small town, but this was one major zombie square dance. If one fell, the others walked right over it. Do-si-do, whoops, smush. Buffy made a face. No doubt about it. Zombies were gross, and they were rude.

The newcomers moved to join the others at the dead folks jamboree, and the walls began to bulge with the pressure. The gate hinges and chains screeched even louder, close to snapping. They were going to get out. Buffy wrinkled her nose. Zombies, meet Slayer. Slayer, stop zombies from feasting on the neighbors.

"I am definitely going to need a bath after this," she muttered, and leaped over the heads of her fan club, smack into the middle of the graveyard. Since almost everybody was pushing against the walls, Buffy could warm up with the stragglers and the newly risen who didn't know what the heck was going on.

Yeah, like any of them had a clue.

As if she did. These spooky ooky guys were rising why?

The zombie closest to her wheeled around and came for her, arms stretched forward like a classic sleepwalker. Its eyes were huge and blank. Its jaws opened and shut. But the fact that it had eyes and a jaw meant the guy hadn't been dead too long, so he'd be stronger than the others. Buffy jumped into the air and launched a hard kick at its face. Whiplash; the thing did a one-eighty and keeled right over.

Another zombie approached from behind. She shot her leg out and back, crushing the zombie's ribs, and sent it flying backwards. She nailed another with a fist to the top of its head and it crumpled again.

"Eeuu," she said. Her knuckles were covered with mold and spider webs. Absently she wiped them on her blouse.

Besides being disgusting, zombies were pretty easy to stop. Problems started only when there were a whole lot of them. Like, say, a whole graveyard full. With three quick kicks, Buffy took down as many zombies. She picked up a broken headstone and smashed in their skulls.

Now the silent majority had begun to realize something tasty was in their midst. Their heads rose. They looked like dogs sniffing the air or high school boys at the Bronze. They started to turn.

They began to advance on her.

"Giles," Buffy said under her breath, "this would be a good time to show up with some special zombie-stopping gear or spells or something." To the zombies, she bellowed—loud enough to startle, if not wake, the dead—"Simon says go back in your graves."

They kept coming. Some wore ragged shrouds, others had on rotting business suits and dresses. One was dressed like a clown, and that one gave her the wiggins worst of all.

"Yo, zombie guys, pay attention," she said, smashing her fist into the chest of one without looking at it, kicking at another, flipping backwards over a third. "When it's Simon says, that means you have to do what I say. Let's be more direct. The Slayer says, die, like, forever."

Still more zombies stumbled toward her. She whirled in a circle, completely surrounded. She heard the click of their jaws opening and shutting. The moaning continued, grew louder now, and really started to bother her. She could feel it in her bones, an ache, a rattle, a weariness. The moans were this extreme wall of sadness, and if that's how being dead made you feel, Buffy figured it was even worse than high school.

Her heart was pounding. She had this mental picture of them overtaking her, cracking her skull open like a coconut, and eating her brains. There were just too many of them. Besides, a lot of the ones she managed to mangle got back up.

"Hey, look, my brains aren't that special, okay?" she said, half-pleading. "I'm flunking history. You don't want them."

A zombie woman in the tatters of a wedding dress grabbed her arm. Buffy fought it off just as another zombie, this one in the remnants of a tuxedo, grabbed her other arm. She threw that one off, too.

"Have you two met before?" she asked, as the zombies collided with each other and fell to the ground. "Like, on the altar?"

Then the clown trudged toward her. Its orange fright wig sat askew on its head, and pieces of gray hair escaped from beneath it. Beneath caked and moldering white clown makeup and a huge, gaping grin, the face was vaguely familiar. There was something about it that reminded her of someone.

It came closer. And closer.

Someone she had seen recently . . .

It opened wide.

The hair stood up on the back of Buffy's neck.

"Mr. O'Leary?" she cried at the zombie clown as she backed up into the arms of another zombie, who began to squeeze her around the middle, hard enough to push the breath out of her lungs.

"I'm comin', darlin' girl!" a man's voice cried.

As the zombie clown lurched toward her and grabbed her around the throat, Mr. O'Leary—as alive as she was, and probably for just as long—dropped down from the cemetery wall and barreled toward her.

"Oh, no," Buffy groaned breathlessly. "Mr. O'Leary, get out of here."

"'Tis a good thing I decided to come back. I'll save you!" he shouted, pushing a zombie from his path.

About a third of the zombies, smelling fresh meat, headed for him. The clown zombie kept strangling Buffy as he tried to get his mouth around the side of her head for that first dainty chomp.

"Giles," she said through gritted teeth, "now's a good time."

Or not.

"Okay, Giles, the plan is?" Xander asked anxiously, as the female vampire Willow and Xander had been calling Red body-slammed the double entry doors of Sunnydale High School for an estimated one hundred and first time.

Thus far the vampires had not been able to enter, which made Giles suspect they could not. Perhaps it was because they hadn't been invited over the threshold. On the other hand, it was clear that Red was alone now. Her partner, whom Willow and Xander had referred to as Blue Eyes, had stopped pounding on the door, and they hadn't heard him shouting for a minute or two.

In addition, Giles was not certain Blue Eyes and Red were alone or if they were all barred from entrance into the school. At any moment, one could come crashing through the doors. In fact, they might already be sneaking down the corridors, intent upon ambushing the three humans.

The time for research was over, Giles knew. The time for action was upon him. Things like this had never occurred back in London. He'd been rather excited to discover he was to be the Watcher of the Slayer. Oh, the misspent enthusiasms of the innocent. Or the ignorant.

"We're coming for you," Red cooed. "You most of all, Xander."

"She knows my name," Xander blurted, obviously even more terrified than before.

Willow, at Giles's side, said with mock concern, "Oh, dear. Now she can look you up in the phone book."

"We're unlisted," Xander said, as if the thought afforded him some measure of relief.

Giles had been holding the journal of Timothy Cassidy. Now he put the book beside the crossbow he had planned to bring to Buffy, gathered the two teenagers closer, and dropped his voice to a whisper.

"Right," he began. "It appears these two at least cannot come inside without an invitation. This is what we'll do. We'll uncover all the windows in the library. Then we'll lure them in and seal them up. When the sun rises, we'll let it do our work for us."

"Solar-powered death-dealing," Xander said, nodding. "Cool. Lure them in how?"

"Seal them up how?" Willow added.

Both the youngsters looked at him with trusting, inquisitive expressions. After all, one might suppose a Watcher would have instant answers to questions such as these.

In which case, one would be sadly mistaken.

"Yes, well, I've been mulling that over." He pushed up his glasses again and gave a thought to Buffy. He was very worried about her. Each moment he wasted dithering in indecision was a moment that could cost her life.

"All right." He nodded at them reassuringly and picked up a canvas sack full of supplies. "I've some things in here that vampires aren't fond of—garlic bulbs, crosses, holy water. Along with some other items I've collected for Buffy." He opened the sack and showed them four pieces of wood like broken tree branches with the bark still on. "To kill Samhain, the Slayer must—"

"Uh, Giles? No offense, but just in case, can we go into that later?" Xander asked.

"Xander, be polite," Willow said, poking the boy in the ribs.

"I said No offense," Xander murmured defensively.

"None taken, I assure you." Giles cleared his throat as he handed Willow the sack. He hesitated a moment as he worked on his plan. Willow and Xander traded worried glances. Giles's sense of responsibility weighed on him ever more heavily.

"You two go to the library and tear the draperies off the windows, then put a cross on each one. We'll just have to hope they either don't notice what you're doing, or don't care. Then we'll get them into the library, block their way out with garlic and holy water, and in the morning, the sun will rise and," he snapped his fingers, "two dead vampires."

"Neato keeno." Xander snapped his fingers in response. "Will, let's go."

"Wait." Willow frowned at Giles. "How are we going to get them into the library?"

Giles nodded. "Right. I shall invite them in and allow them to chase me. You two hide. Once we're in the library, I'll get out somehow and then you two scatter the garlic and water over the threshold before they can follow."

Willow shook her head. "I was with you—sort of—until the somehow part."

Xander crossed his arms. "Yes. Somehow is the part where I also feel challenged about moving forward. Also, the part where they chase you."

"Well, all right, then, have you a better plan?" Giles looked at each of them in turn. "In that case, we'll go with mine."

"But, Giles," Willow said anxiously, "you're the Watcher. Buffy needs you. If you die, she'll probably get killed."

"But if one of *us* dies," Xander went on, "she'll totally feel bad." He raised his hand. "I say we vote on Giles's plan. See, Giles, we live in a democracy," he added. "We vote on stuff."

"To my knowledge, the pursuit of the vampires is not part of your Constitution," Giles countered.

"Neither is pursuit by the vampires," Willow said firmly.

"Or for the vampires." Xander nodded wisely.

Giles blinked. There were times when he appreciated the rather esoteric babble of the average American adolescent, and if pressed, he would have to admit that he found Xander Harris and Willow Rosenberg to be above average in many respects. Studying not being one of them in Xander's case, however, but that was beside the point. He found their strong sense of loyalty to each other and to the Slayer most admirable, and he was touched by their concern for his welfare.

However, returning to the notion of babbling, he was beginning to feel cast adrift in this conversation. In short, they were losing him, and he was just about to inform them of that fact, when they both nodded at him.

"We don't like it, but we'll do it your way," Willow said.

"Oh," Giles said, surprised. "Good."

"If you promise to take a cross and holy water," Willow added. She shrugged uncertainly. "I guess if you have garlic with you they might not follow you."

He looked at each of them in turn and said, "And I assume each of you will carry a cross on your person?"

"We're armed and loaded for bear," Xander assured him, as he took a cross out of the sack and held it up for inspection. "Whatever that means. Watch as I exhibit my ignorance."

"It's a hunting reference," Willow observed, also holding up a cross. "Bears. Rifles. Bullets."

"Okay. Cool. Ignorance resolved. But I move on," Xander said. "I get the part where vampires can't come into your house if you don't invite them in. But that's, like, your house. Your territory. What about public buildings? Like, um, schools?"

Willow looked worried. "I can't remember. Have we ever seen a vampire at the movies? Or in a grocery store?"

The three looked at one another.

Further discussion was curtailed by the shattering of a window somewhere inside the school.

"Not the answer I was looking for," Willow said anxiously. Her eyes widened. "Giles?"

"Run," Giles said, fishing in his pocket for his keys. "I shall detain them for as long as I can."

Xander grabbed her hand. "Giles, if you are . . . *way* detained, what do we tell Buffy?"

"Take the crossbow," Giles began, then realized there wasn't enough time to go through everything. "The Watcher's Journal," he said, handing the volume to Willow. "Timothy Cassidy's. Be sure to take that with you, too."

Footsteps pounded down the corridor.

"For God's sake, run!" Giles shouted.

The two dashed around a corner and disappeared.

"Xan-der," came the teasing whisper of Red, the vampire female who'd set her sights on the young man.

Giles began to run, too.

In the direction of the voice.

"No, no!" Mr. O'Leary shouted. "Sean!"

He jumped on the back of the clown zombie and pounded on its head and arms, trying to stop it from strangling Buffy. "It's me own dead brother!"

Explaining why the clown looked so familiar, Buffy realized as she started to lose consciousness from lack of air. She'd thought it was Mr. O'Leary himself, somehow, as impossible as that would have been. Or maybe she thought she recognized the clown from one of those childhood nightmares called magic shows at kiddie birthday parties. She hated them.

Clowns wigged her . . .

. . . and ventriloquist's dummies . . .

. . . and dying . . .

. . . and raisins . . . raisin bran . . . something about raisin brain.

Raisin brains . . .

. . . risin' brains . . .

"No!" she shouted, gathering her strength as Mr. O'Leary managed to damage his brother enough for Buffy to break his grasp. She tucked in her head and collapsed to the ground. She heaved in huge gasps of air, fighting against blacking out, and kicked backwards, shattering the knee of the zombie who'd had her around the waist. In front of her, Mr. O'Leary tumbled to the ground with the walking, clown-suited corpse of his brother.

Mr. O'Leary was pinned beneath the flailing clown zombie.

Buffy leaped to her feet and started kicking zombie parts as fast and hard as she could.

"This is—I mean, was—your brother?" she asked, horrified.

Mr. O'Leary rolled from beneath the clown and struggled to get to his feet. "Alas, dead these sixteen years. I'll tell you this. He was not buried in a clown costume. Someone has done this out of spite."

"This must be hard for you," she said, huffing. She yanked Mr. O'Leary up and slammed her fist into another zombie who attempted to grab on to the man. "Now, please, get out of here," she said.

"I'll stay and fight with you," he insisted.

"Go to the school. Ask Mr. Giles the librarian to come as fast as he can." She thought of Willow and Xander. Surely, if they'd made it to the library, they'd be here with Giles by now. "He can help."

"I'll not be leaving you here alone!" Mr. O'Leary insisted.

Suddenly, he cried out, grabbed at his chest, and fell to the ground. The zombies swarmed over Buffy, and she thrashed at them, breaking free. But it was getting harder and harder to move.

The Slayer was getting tired.

CHAPTER 7

As Giles ran toward the voice of the female vampire, her companion, fully attired in a cowboy costume, jumped out from around a corner.

"Howdy, pardner," he said to Giles, who halted immediately, whirled around, and ran toward the library as fast as he could.

It was not fast enough.

Blue Eyes was upon him, jumping on Giles's back as if he were a horse. He kicked at Giles's sides and yelled, "Yee-ha!"

Taking his cue from his training sessions with the Slayer, Giles tucked in his head and leaned forward. The vampire flew over his head and sprawled on the ground.

"I can't take you anywhere," Red drawled at Blue Eyes in mock disgust.

Giles threw himself against the wall and held out

his cross, brandishing it from side to side as the female vampire slowed to a walk and smiled at Giles. Blue Eyes got up and moved in on him from the opposite direction.

"You don't need that, Deputy," Red said sweetly. "Just put it down."

"Stay back." Giles reached in his pocket and uncapped the holy water. He wasn't certain how to play this out. This was what the Americans charmingly called a Mexican standoff. Each of the three of them had a weapon, and as long as none of them made the first move, they were stuck here indefinitely. But if he ran again, they would surely overtake him.

As Giles watched in horror, the two vampires transformed into the hideous creatures they truly were, the faces they wore when the hunger was upon them. They licked their fangs and swiped their clawed hands menacingly at him, hissing. Giles swallowed hard and stood his ground. The Slayer faced such danger daily; he could do no less when called upon to save her.

"You're the little Slayer's Watcher," Red said. "The Master has promised a reward for your heart. We'll make you die slowly. Painfully."

"We should take him to the Master alive," Blue Eyes cut in, averting his eyes as Giles tilted the cross slightly in his direction. "Our reward will be even greater."

"I'm sorry to disappoint you, but neither of you is going anywhere," Giles said.

Red's laughter seemed to echo down the corridor. "Your arm will tire soon," she said.

She began to sit down on the floor when Xander called, "Yo, Giles! Do we have any books on interior decorating?" It was the cue that they had finished pulling down the curtains and adorning the windows with crosses.

Red's hideous face broke into an enormous smile. "My dear Xander must be in the library."

"With my girlfriend," Blue Eyes agreed, grinning.

They looked at Giles, who made his eyes move left, away from the library, as a ruse.

"It's this way," Blue Eyes said, pointing left, skirting around Giles and joining Red. "We'll take the kids by surprise and come back for him."

They loped down the corridor in the wrong direction, as Giles had planned, the two laughing horribly. Giles took off toward the library.

"Xander! Willow! I'm coming!" he shouted, and behind him, the vampires called out to each other and turned to give chase. Giles redoubled his efforts, running as fast as he could, and flew toward the open library door. Blue Eyes and Red were perhaps three or four feet behind him. Giles sailed over the threshold and was immediately yanked to one side by Xander.

The vampires passed over the threshold.

Willow darted from the other side of the door and tossed open vials of holy water at them, holding a cross in her hand. Their faces began to smoke as they howled in pain and covered their eyes.

Xander pulled Giles out of the library and tossed a pair of crosses behind them. Willow hopped over them, sprinkling the floor and doors with holy water.

"We'll get you for this!" Red cried, lowering her hands to her sides. Her face was a smoking mess; she looked as if she was wearing a Halloween fright mask that had melted. She started toward them and screamed as her foot came down on a cross.

Willow pulled the double doors shut with the vampires hissing at her, then wrapped strands of garlic bulbs around the door handles. Similar strands were on the inside handles as well.

"Let's go," Giles said, and he, Xander, and Willow raced down the corridors and passages of Sunnydale High. Giles hoped that the trap had worked, but now was not the time to verify it. At the least, they had bought themselves some time.

He hoped they had bought Buffy time as well.

They reached the front doors, his books, and the crossbow. Willow still held the canvas sack. Wonderful girl. She had kept her head.

Xander pushed open the door and said, "What if there are more of them out here?"

"Ever the optimist," Willow retorted. "I'm holding the bag, why don't you make yourself useful and grab the crossbow?"

"Don't we need arrows?" Xander asked, as he hefted the weapon.

"They take bolts. Which there are. It's all right," Willow replied.

They gathered up the supplies and raced out of the school and down the stone steps.

Buffy gritted her teeth, wishing for anything that could drown out the way depressing, Cobain-inspiring moaning of the zombies. Mr. O'Leary was dead. Buffy knew that just from looking at him. And it wasn't from any zombie attack. The poor old guy had just up and died. The cardiac police had come along and cuffed him. Heart attack city.

Not that she was in any position to do anything about it.

As she defended herself, several of the zombies latched on to Mr. O'Leary's corpse. She tried to protect it—him—but saving her own bacon was hard enough. The Slayer looked away, she didn't want to see what would happen to the old man's corpse when the dead guys got their choppers going.

A zombie grabbed her shoulder, and as she spun to crush its face, she saw what they'd done with Mr. O'Leary. Nothing like what she expected. He'd been hung up in a large pepper tree in the center of the cemetery, where he dangled like a horrible scarecrow. Scarecrow. Coincidence, or nasty inspiration? She'd no idea, but had to assume they only liked really-truly-alive folks. As a fellow dead guy, Mr. O'Leary didn't meet their culinary needs, and was tossed out like garbage. She only hoped the sweetly crazy old man didn't rise again.

Buffy didn't want to have to fight him.

She turned away. Buffy didn't want to see any more.

The zombie moaning started up again, and the shambling dead began to crawl to their feet once more. Buffy glanced quickly around and realized that there were still dozens upon dozens of them moving. Hungry. Not good. She had to destroy their brains to kill them, if the movie rules applied. And she just couldn't concentrate that much with so many bony fingers clawing at her.

And that noise! It was enough to make that happy mailman on Mr. Rogers go postal!

Giles hadn't arrived. Willow and Xander might be dead for all Buffy knew. She wanted to get out of the cemetery, find them, make sure they were all right. Then they could all come back, Giles could find some anti-zombie spells in one of his smelly books, and they could gorge on whatever Halloween candy was left at her house.

"Nice fantasy, Summers," she whispered to herself. She had to get out of there first.

Buffy turned and started for the gates, slamming her open palm into the nose of a nearby zombie, sending bone splinters into its brain. It fell over a headstone and didn't move again, and she figured if she could pull that maneuver on all of them, she'd be in good shape. Problem was, when they started to move in, she didn't have time to aim.

And they *were* moving in. In fact . . .

There were so many hungry zombies stacked up at the walls and in front of the gates that Buffy just couldn't see how she was going to get out without shutting them all down. Which could take, oh, the rest of her life. However long that was.

"Look, folks," she said nervously, growing truly frightened now as they closed in on her, a wall of dead flesh and bone. "It's been a heck of a fiesta, y'know? But, really, I turn into a pumpkin at midnight."

Buffy pulled the broken nose trick on two more zombies, then elbowed another in the chest. The dead man's chest collapsed, and the stink from the corpse almost made her throw up.

Being the Slayer didn't mean that Buffy wasn't afraid of the things she faced. Only that she was confident in her ability to overcome them. Most of the time. But when that confidence failed, she was still a sixteen-year-old girl who wanted very much to keep breathing.

She glanced around nervously, and noticed something odd at the rear of the cemetery. Something that hadn't seemed significant before because it didn't threaten her life. While the sides and front of the cemetery had high walls, the back was bordered by farmland. The only thing separating the graveyard from the fields beyond was a three-foot-high stone wall that looked as if it had been there since man discovered fire. Or at least the gas grill.

The reason she hadn't noticed it was because there weren't any zombies back there. None. Zero. Nada. Now, sure, the more residential sections of Sunnydale had more people, which to the headsuckers meant more brains to eat. But she couldn't believe none of them had realized they could just step over that wall and be out of the cemetery.

Not that it mattered. What mattered was it was a way out. Not too many zombies between Buffy and the field.

"I'll be back," she said in her gruffest Terminator voice. Then she ripped an arm from a particularly decrepit looking zombie and used it to shatter the skulls of two others. Then she was bounding from grave marker to tombstone to the roof of a crypt. She held on to the wings of a carved marble angel, and looked toward the low stone wall again. Not far away. Not too many zombies.

No problem.

Buffy dropped down to the ground again, and immediately bony fingers began reaching for her. The moaning had reached a fever pitch, as if they knew she was going to escape them. A part of her wanted to slow, to surrender, to ease their pain. That's how much of a downer their vocals were.

Instead, she kicked, punched, and elbowed her way toward the field. A high, spinning kick actually beheaded one of the zombies, and Buffy was psyched to see that she only had another thirty yards or so to go.

Twenty.

Ten.

Dead fingers twined in her hair, yanking her backwards off her feet. Zombies came down on top of her, jaws clacking as they tried to bite into her. The moaning became too much.

Buffy closed her eyes, a tear beginning to form. Too much.

Her heart raced. Then a fire exploded in her gut and roared its way up into her throat to blast out of her as a scream.

"Nooooooooo!" she cried, and surged upward with incredible strength. Zombies went flying like bowling pins, save for one or two that she shook off as she turned to run, wide eyed and terrified, for the stone wall.

Then she was there. Buffy dove over the wall, rolled into a somersault, and sprang to her feet again. She felt something in her hair and batted at it, the remains of dead flesh torn from fingers as she struggled against a dead man's grip. Buffy pulled the flesh away, then wiped her hand on her pants in disgust. She panted, trying to catch her breath, then glanced around to see which way would be best for her escape. The zombies would be after her . . .

Zombies. After her.

Not.

They weren't coming after her at all. It gave her the wiggins, but they just stood there on the other side of the stone wall and moaned, staring at her out of withered eyes like raisins—there, she knew there was a reason she didn't like raisins!—or empty sockets.

"Okay!" Buffy said, confused but pleased. "You

guys and gals just hang out here, and I'll go find someone who will know how we can lullaby you all back to death."

She looked at them one last time, shivered off the wiggins that was creeping up on her, and turned to walk along next to the wall. If she circled around the cemetery, she'd get back to the street. Then she'd have a long walk to school to find Giles.

Once more, she worried for Willow and Xander.

Buffy had an odd sensation, a familiar one. In fact, she'd felt it earlier that same night. As if she was being watched. As if some Peeping Tom was checking her out in the girls' locker room. As if someone was sneaking up on her . . .

The Slayer spun, ready to attack, poised to take on any zombies that had finally come over the wall for her.

There was nobody there.

Buffy took a deep breath, let it out, and wrote off her jitters as the result of a very long, majorly tiring Halloween night. Somewhere off in Sunnydale, the church bells began to toll midnight.

"Great," she muttered. "The witching hour has begun. As if this night hasn't been enough of a drag."

She began to turn, to start for the street again, but something caught her eye in the moonlight. Up the hill, a cross jutted from the ground, silhouetted in the moonlight. Not a cross, she realized, but a post with a bar nailed near the top.

Her stomach sank and churned and burned. Then

went deathly cold. Every muscle in Buffy's body tensed, as true, rabid fear coursed through her. There had been a scarecrow on that post earlier, she was certain. She had seen it from outside the cemetery. But now . . . Where had it gone? Where could it have gone?

It had rained all day, Halloween rain. And Willow and Xander had warned her about Halloween rain and scarecrows, and not trespassing on the fields they watched over.

Sure, reason enough for a serious wiggins, but not for the fear she felt now. Horrible. Terror like nothing she'd ever known. It was almost enough to make her want to curl up in a ball there in the field. It wasn't natural. It was some kind of . . .

". . . magic," she whispered.

But it didn't matter. She was terrified. So much so that she didn't want to walk all the way along the cemetery to get to the street. She was willing, even happy, to make a beeline right through the zombie-shambling-room-only cemetery to get away from this field. Besides, she just realized that she had left her Slayer's bag somewhere in the cemetery.

Buffy launched herself toward the zombies, toward the stone wall—and slammed into something hard and unyielding. She smacked her forehead against it, had the breath knocked out of her, and was thrown back to the ground.

Now she knew why the zombies weren't coming into the field. They couldn't. And whatever was keeping them out was now keeping her in. She was trapped. Her breathing sped up, her terror growing by the instant.

Somewhere up the hill, she heard a low, hissing voice. Please, maybe it's only the wind!

It called to her.

"Sssslayer!"

CHAPTER 8

Willow stared out the passenger window of the Gilesmobile as they raced toward the cemetery. Xander, in the back, scanned through the rear window. Somewhere in the distance, thunder rumbled and the air seemed to fill with moisture again.

Willow shivered, chilled through to her bones. The rain had stopped, but now she wondered if it wasn't going to start all over again. Still, the chill she felt wasn't from the weather, but the horrible fear and dread that was creeping over her.

"I don't think it was an act of nature that shut the phone lines down," Giles observed as he stepped on the gas.

Willow stirred and shivered harder. "I'm thinking supernature," she agreed, as she glanced in the rearview mirror. "Something didn't want Buffy to contact you."

Nervously she played with the frayed edge of Giles's canvas bag o' tricks.

"You know," Willow said hopefully, "one of the vampires at the Bronze told Buffy they had the night off. I wonder if that's true. We haven't come across anything diabolical since we three left the school."

Maybe it was all over because Buffy had killed the pumpkin king, Samhain. Maybe Halloween was over forever.

Xander looked away from the window long enough to drawl, "Yeah, well, he's the same vampire she dusted for unauthorized snacking not five minutes later. And don't forget our own private posse, Will. Those being the escapees of the dude ranch from hell who wanted to corral us three."

"Roy Rogers and Dale Evans," Giles observed. Willow and Xander looked at him blankly. "Popular American cowpeople. I was referring to your Red and Blue Eyes, and their Halloween, um, getups."

"Cowpeople?" Willow quickly covered her mouth, but she knew Giles saw her quick grin. It amazed her that she could grin at a time like this, but that's what hanging with Buffy did for—or to—you. You developed a strange sense of humor to keep from going bonkers when confronted by horrors you thought existed only in movies. It was kind of like surviving high school. At least, that was how it was for her.

"Hey, I know about those cowpeople," Xander

piped up. "They had a horse named Trigger that they stuffed after he died."

"Okay, that's gross," Willow said, thinking uncomfortably of the many pets she had had in her life. She couldn't imagine keeping them around like strange dead trophies. Willow cast Giles a sidelong glance. "Were these people in one of your dusty-demon books for mummifying their pony?"

Giles shook his head. "No. They were quite famous, in their day. Which clearly is not your day. As for the stuffing, they put the horse in their museum, I believe." He pushed up his glasses. "They had a famous theme song. It began, 'Happy trails to you . . .'"

Giles stopped, apparently distracted.

"He trailed off," Willow said. "Don't abandon us now, Giles, we were just reveling in your magnificent tenor."

Giles sniffed, stared out past the windshield. "Let me tell you what we must do to help the Slayer. To begin . . ."

"He trailed off again," Xander said.

"What's wrong, Giles?" Willow asked, peering at him, as he put a foot on the brake.

"Mr. Rupert, sir?" Xander queried.

Wordlessly, Giles raised a hand and pointed through the windshield.

The wrought-iron entrance to the cemetery rose like a strange flower in the moonlit sky. A broken tree drooped behind it.

From the tree hung a human body.

"No," Willow groaned. "It can't be." She swallowed down her terror and wrenched open the car door.

"Willow, wait," Giles called, but she was out of the car before he had completely stopped it. She stumbled, kept running. Her chest was so tight she could hardly move. Certainly, she had been afraid for Buffy before, but it had never really sunk in that Buffy might actually be killed. That they could go on with their lives minus the best friend she had ever had. That the forces of evil might win.

How could she go on without Buffy? How could any of them go on knowing that the Slayer had . . . had lost?

"Buffy," she cried, and ran through the open gates.

She stumbled to a stop and burst into quick tears of relief. It wasn't Buffy. It was Mr. O'Leary.

Or what was left of him.

Willow stared at his corpse a moment, then tore her gaze away. Priorities.

"Buffy?" Willow called.

By the time she got hold of herself, Giles and Xander had caught up with her. Giles carried his sack and Xander had the crossbow. Both of them stared up at the dead man.

"Oh, my God," Xander said. His face was chalk white.

"It gets worse," Willow said, and tugged on Xander's hand.

"I hate worse," Xander grumbled, and turned to peer into the darkness across the cemetery where Willow was pointing. "What, are the headstones moving?"

"Those aren't headstones," Giles said. "Those are zombies. The walking dead."

Suddenly, as if someone had given the zombies their cue, they began to moan. It was a horrible, starving, desperate sound that hit Willow like a fist. She staggered under the grief and despair, almost unable to remain standing. There were dozens of them, maybe hundreds, all making the same awful noise.

They were crowded together at the far end of the cemetery. Willow was relieved to see that they didn't even seem aware that she, Giles, and Xander were nearby.

Then it was as if they had heard her thoughts. A cluster off to the right pivoted slowly to look at the newly arrived alive people. Some of the dead guys began to stumble toward them. The rest were like a writhing, rotten wall of flesh as they stood facing outward, lined up against the back wall as they stared and moaned.

"Isn't that Mr. Flutie?" Willow asked, first staring and then purposely turning away from the half chewed up corpse shambling toward them.

"They're stuck in here," Xander shouted, covering his ears. "It must be bumming them out. That's why they're moaning."

"No. They've gotten out at the back," Giles shouted, pointing, but Willow was too short to see whatever it was he saw. "They're grouping along the perimeter of that field."

"Field?" Willow and Xander cried at the same time.

"But they're not going in," Giles mused. "Odd."

"Is there a scarecrow? Do you see a scarecrow?" Willow demanded anxiously.

"I don't see one," Giles said loudly after a minute. "But clearly they can't go into the field."

Xander tapped Willow on the shoulder. "What?" she asked, craning to see. "Is there one? Xander?"

He tapped her again.

"Xander, just tell me."

She began to turn, then realized Xander was standing slightly in front of her to the right. He couldn't be tapping her shoulder. She whirled around.

A zombie with one eye lunged at her. It grabbed her arm and pulled her toward itself; its mouth opened wide and a worm slithered out.

"Willow!" Giles shouted. He yanked her away and swung the sack at the zombie's head.

As the three looked on, the sack crushed the zombie's skull and it sank to the ground.

"Back up," Giles ordered, as three more zombies lurched toward them.

The zombies split up, one coming for each of them. The undead buddy system.

Xander said, "Okay, the plan is modified to?"

"Oh, dear," Giles said. "Back up."

"We need a plan B, Giles," Willow cried.

"That *is* plan B!" Giles said in frustration.

Somehow, in the short time the three had spent inside the cemetery gates, zombies had completely surrounded them. Their moaning reached fever pitch. Then over their awful groans came a strangely soft but audible hiss.

"Sssslayer."

The sound made the hair stand up on Willow's neck. It spoke of pure evil and hatred and death.

"It came from the field," Xander said into her ear as he darted a glance over his shoulder toward the back of the cemetery.

One of the zombies swiped at Willow. She jumped back, then spun around to see that more of the zombies who had been standing along the back wall were turning in the direction of those present and accounted for with living, pulsing brains.

"Buffy might be in that field," Xander went on. "Will, it's been raining, and Buffy may be in a field."

Then Xander made a face. He said, "Um, incoming info fact: the bar has just been raised on the possibility of Buffy's presence in that field."

He pointed at something.

"Why do you think that she—" Willow began, then saw Buffy's Slayer's bag next to a headstone near the wall.

"Isn't it great to have twenty-twenty?" Xander asked, not happily.

Willow bellowed, "Giles, we have to get to her."

"Getting to her. There's plan B," Xander agreed, as he dodged his zombie dance partner. "But a notion here. Getting to her alive with our brains still in our heads is even better. And the way we do that is?"

No answer.

"Come on, Giles!" Willow said frantically. "It's shambling room only in here."

"There are too many of them for us to fight," Giles observed, swinging at his zombie. His fist connected and the zombie tumbled to the ground. Its legs and feet still moved as if it were walking. "We've got to fend them off until I can figure something out."

"What?" Willow made a fist and grimaced as a zombie in a moldy black priest's garb stumbled in her direction. Its mouth opened and closed, making its jaw do the Rice Krispies snap-crackle-pop. There was nothing in its sightless gaze to suggest it had a mind, and that made it all the more frightening. Vampires and werewolves could be talked to, possibly outwitted. But these witless wonders would keep coming until they were physically stopped. And the Three Musketeers did not have the physics to make that happen.

"Buffy," Willow called as loudly as she could. Her

voice shook. "Buffy, we're coming as soon as we can!"

"Buffy!"

It was Willow's voice. Coming from the grave-yard. Where the zombies were. Not good.

"Willow, are you okay?" Buffy shouted back. "Is Giles with you? Is Xander okay?"

"There are so many of them!" Willow called. "We're trying to get to you. We found your Slayer's bag and Giles has some things he thinks will help you!"

"No, stay away!" Buffy ordered her, waving her hands in case they could see her. "I can't get to you, but stay out of here."

Buffy pushed against the invisible barrier, way wigged. Hordes of moaning zombies pushed on the other side. If it should give way when she didn't expect it, she'd be a nice midnight snack. The zombie equivalent of raiding the fridge. But what was happening to her friends?

"Get out of there!" she cried frantically.

"We can't. We've been boxed in," Willow said.

Then Willow screamed.

"Willow? Willow! Xander? Giles?" Buffy threw herself at the barrier. She had been terrified moments earlier by the voice she had heard, by the presence she had felt there in the field with her. Now that terror was overwhelmed by her fear for her friends. She kicked and pounded, getting nowhere. All she heard was moaning.

Then Giles said loudly, "Buffy, stay where you are. I'm working on the problem."

"Which one?" she called. "The barrier, or the zombies, or—"

"Ssslayer."

The single word sizzled across the back of Buffy's neck like a piece of dry ice. She began shivering so hard she thought she might be sick. She couldn't explain it, but there was something in that voice that frightened her more than any horror she had ever faced.

"Ssslayer, come."

Buffy whirled around and scanned the horizon. To the left was the rise of the hill and the empty cross-shape that had once held a scarecrow. To her right, the ground was dotted with rows of trees. Then the hill fell away into a valley, and there was a box-shape at the bottom. A building of some sort.

Black clouds began to tumble one over the other, threatening to cover the pale moon. Buffy had the distinct feeling she was being watched, by someone besides her peanut gallery of reanimated corpses. She swallowed down the knot in her throat and glanced from side to side. She could hardly breathe.

"Sorry, I'll pass on that invite," she called out as firmly as she could, but her voice shook.

The answer was a low, cruel laugh that seemed to slither up toward her from the valley. She peered into the night. The field was gloomy and dark, and the ground was soaked from the earlier rains.

There were pumpkins everywhere. She was in a pumpkin field.

Xander and Willow had warned her not to walk in any fields. By coming in here, she had set them up for chowtime and landed herself in a trap.

"Come, or they die."

She could think of nothing to say. No clever retort sprang to mind. No silly remark. It was as if everything was sliding away from her and she was balancing at the edge of a cliff. She took a step forward and tripped over something stretched across the earth. Before she could catch herself, she fell to her hands and knees into thick mud and tangles of vines.

The sense of being watched grew even stronger. As she lifted her head, the vines between her fingers seemed to tighten. She peered down at the earth.

A small, round pumpkin swiveled as she moved her head. She blinked, lurched forward, raised her fist, and crashed it down on the pumpkin. It caved in and began to roll down the hill.

Laughter filled Buffy's ears, low and cunning and eager.

"Come."

"Willow, can you hear me?" Buffy called, ignoring the voice.

There was no answer.

Then Buffy realized she no longer heard the moaning of the zombies. She heard nothing but her heartbeat. Struggling, she got to her feet.

"Giles?" she called.

No answer. The voice had told her, essentially, to follow the bouncing pumpkin. Down into a valley. Where she couldn't see a thing. Instead, she turned left and started climbing the hill.

Suddenly, like huge plumes of smoke, more clouds raced across the moon. They were gigantic, more like a thick web than clouds, and before she realized what was happening, Buffy was plunged into complete blackness.

She took a breath and kept walking. She thought of her Slayer's bag back in the cemetery, and all the goodies it contained—stakes, matches, candles—and realized that she was basically defenseless except for her strength and her reflexes. At least the others might be able to make use of the things in her bag, she thought. At least they weren't as defenseless as she was.

"So *not* defenseless," she muttered. "I'm the Slayer."

Something crackled behind her. She whirled around in an attack stance. She could see nothing. She moved her hands in front of herself, to each side, waved them behind herself. She felt nothing.

A bolt of lightning cracked across the sky, lighting up the field.

A dozen pumpkins were fanned in a semicircle behind her. She didn't know if they had actually moved or if they had lain in the field that way, but she slammed as many as she could down the hill as the light faded.

Another crack of lightning spiked through the blackness.

Buffy spun to face the hill.

At the crest, in the brilliance, a figure loomed. The way he stood, the flash of light gave her just a glimpse of his body, his head still blanketed by darkness. He wore overalls and a dark, ragged shirt. His hands were on his hips and his feet were encased in cast-off work boots. His hands were made of straw.

She took a step backwards.

Lightning cracked a third time.

She saw his face.

She opened her mouth to scream, but no sound would come out.

His head was a huge, rotting pumpkin. Green flame licked out of jagged carved eyes, which shifted and squinted as he looked down on her. A nightmare jack-o'-lantern, the pumpkin head leered at her, hideous and savage. Its mouth—lined with horrible fangs—was pulled into a broad smile so wide it disappeared around the sides of the blistered gourd.

It belched sickly green fire from its mouth and carved nostrils, flames shot from its eyes and glowed beneath the orange, uneven skin, casting shadows over its face as it cocked its head, regarding her. Its eyes stared at her, almost spinning. It began to slaver and drool, jagged rows of teeth flashing and slashing as it opened and closed its mouth like a mindless zombie. Licking its chops.

But it—he—was far from mindless. Cunning and

hatred were etched clearly on his face as if someone had carved them there.

He lifted his arms from his sides as if mimicking being hung above the field. Blood dripped from their razor edges.

Blood, black in the green firelight, streamed from his mouth.

He threw back his head and whispered, *"Happy Halloween."* Though the sound was a whisper, it echoed over the field.

"Off to see the Wizard," Buffy muttered, and began to back up.

CHAPTER 9

As Buffy backed away from the hideous pumpkin-headed scarecrow, she found herself thinking simply, This is it. This is when the Slayer crashes and burns.

How else to explain the complete and total horror that had seized her and throttled her like the scarecrow's blood-drenched hand around her throat? She couldn't stop staring at him. She couldn't turn her back on him and run, though all her Slayer's training—and her own personal wish to keep living—told her that that was exactly what she must do. Some misfiring instinct for self-preservation insisted that she not take her gaze off him, not for a second. To look away was to die.

But if she didn't get moving, that was exactly what was going to happen.

The pumpkins behind Buffy began to laugh.

Something nudged her boot. She kicked at it without looking.

It bit her through the leather.

"Ow!" she cried involuntarily.

The pumpkin-headed scarecrow looked down on her.

"Do you think that hurt?" he demanded. *"That is nothing compared to the pain you will feel when I rip out your beating heart."*

Buffy swallowed hard. She wanted to say, "Samhain, I presume," to sound smart and unafraid, but all that came out was his name. "Samhain."

"Slayer."

Samhain extended his arm toward her and beckoned for her to approach. It was not difficult to stand her ground. She was paralyzed.

Something else bit her, harder this time. By pure reflex, she kicked at it but did not dare take her eyes away from Samhain.

"Come to me now," Samhain said. *"Join the revel of all the fears of the timeless hours. Of witches and ghouls and demons, of death and pain and dying and the forever blackness you call the Dark Place. Lay your life at my feet and I will give you relief from the soul-killing terror that you feel."*

"I don't feel anything," she insisted weakly.

Samhain smiled, and his head was almost sliced in two by his own fanglike teeth. Blood streamed from his mouth and splattered on the ground.

"You feel everything," he said. *"Every fear you have ever had. Remember when you were very little,*

and the pile of clothes in the corner looked like the bogeyman? Remember how you were certain that your dolls were watching you? That they moved when you looked away? Remember your clothes closet, and how the door would open slowly in the night?" Samhain smiled. *"Remember the nightmare helplessness you felt then?"*

Cold dread washed over her. She did remember.

"My handiwork," he said proudly. *"A monster under your bed. Someone following you home. Someone waiting in the hallway with a knife. I command the fears of your kind. I conjure them up, I smother you with them like a pillow over your face. I make hearts stop. I make Slayers die."*

Buffy shook herself hard as buckets of fear splashed over her. She was trembling violently. She was so afraid. Afraid to move, to breathe.

Afraid to die.

"You will not stop me, girl," Samhain crowed.

Buffy raised her chin. Those fears were no longer childhood nightmares. They were part of her daily life. There really were monsters lying in wait for her. In her reality, evil creatures did live inside dolls and creep under her bed and rise from the dead to wound her and kill her. As afraid of them as she had been, and still was, she faced them and fought them.

And defeated them.

She was the Slayer.

She looked at Samhain with narrowed eyes and said, "Oh, but I will stop you, Mr. Pumpkin Eater. You're not the king of all fear, just of this one night.

And frankly, you're not that much of a king at all. I didn't vote for you."

Samhain shook with fury. The flames shot out of his eyes and mouth and a horrible growl rumbled in his chest, making the earth shake.

"Enough!" he shouted.

Samhain threw open his arms. The skies cracked open and rain poured down.

There was intense, incredible pain at her ankles.

She glanced down. The pumpkins had advanced on her. They were slicing through her boots with jack-o'-lantern teeth. Buffy tried to shake them off, then looked up to see Samhain spring at her like a huge wolf.

Buffy shouted and dropped to the ground. Samhain arced over her head. She whirled around and fell into a battle stance, then smashed her right foot into his midsection as hard as she could.

It was like kicking iron. She fell onto her back, the wind knocked out of her, sheer terror knocked into her. It had been a mistake to touch him. He was evil in solid form. He was the power of fear incarnate.

She had never been more afraid in her life.

As he flung himself at her, she skirted around him and began flying down the hill. She had to get out of here, get away. There was no way to kill fear. And even if there were, she was not going to be the one to do it.

Her Slaying days were over. She had just resigned. She wanted to live.

The rain came down in torrents. She slid and fell a

dozen times in the pitch black, her only light the glowing head of Samhain as he bolted after her. Her hands were bleeding and slick with mud, which the rain sluiced off as she ran for all she was worth.

To her right was the graveyard; she saw some flickering lights and wondered if that was Giles, Willow, and Xander with her Slayer's equipment. She wondered if she would ever see them again.

"You cannot outrun me. You cannot outfight me," Samhain growled after her. She felt icy breath on her neck and ran until she thought her heart might burst.

I make hearts stop, he had said. He had not lied.

Incredibly, huge pumpkins flung themselves at her, pummeling her. Though she realized it must be Samhain's power somehow, it still seemed as though the pumpkins had an evil of their own and moved by their own will. But that couldn't be. It just couldn't!

Within seconds she was bruised and aching and soaked to the bone. Unable to see the pumpkins, she raised her arms to protect her face and continued her run.

She ran into the rows of trees, and thought at first that pumpkins were leaping from them. But they were apple trees, and she was hitting the apples as she ran.

"You cannot defeat me," Samhain added.

"I know, I know, I get it, okay? Class dismissed," Buffy whispered, and kept going.

The ground leveled off; she realized she was at the bottom of the valley. There'd been a building down there. As she stared wildly into the blackness, terrified that at any moment he would catch her, the lightning flashed again.

Dead ahead was the building. It was a barn.

For a moment, her hopes were raised as she instinctively ran toward shelter. Then she realized that he was herding her into it. Once inside, she would be trapped.

She liked to think he would be trapped, too.

But at the last moment, she veered off and ran to the side of the barn. By then the lightning burst had faded, and she was running in torrential rain and utter darkness again.

Behind her, Samhain said, *"I can see you, Slayer. I see every move you make. There's nowhere to hide from the Dark King of Samhuinn."*

Something whipped her knees. After about a minute, she was wading through a field of tall vegetation that brushed around her hips. She glanced over her shoulder.

The glowing ball of Samhain's head was perhaps twenty yards away.

She wondered if he really could see her.

"Help me, someone, please," she whispered, and dropped to her stomach in the tall plants. She lay as still as death and clenched her jaw. The scent of grass rose around her.

And then the scent of the grave, as his heavy footfalls smashed into the tall grass.

"Sssslayer," he called. *"I'm coming for you now."*

She remained unmoving as the rain washed over her. Her mind raced. She had to figure out how to stay alive until morning, or destroy Samhain, or both.

His footsteps shook the ground.

A small furry something with tiny paws and a very long tail crawled over the backs of her hands. She didn't flinch, didn't move a muscle.

He came closer.

And closer.

Without breathing, she waited.

"I will destroy you tonight," he said.

Buffy swallowed hard. Tears streamed down her face. She was afraid, deathly afraid. She couldn't even think, she was so terrified.

As soon as she could no longer hear his footsteps, she got up and blindly ran back toward the orchard. She had no plan, no thought, except to get away from him.

In the cemetery, in the pouring rain, the zombies had surrounded Xander, Willow, and Giles. Xander looked at Willow, who was doing a much better Slayerette job of pounding them than he would have expected, she being, er, a non-guy. But that was so sexist of him.

"Giles, plan C would be good now," he said anxiously as he kicked a zombie in the shins and pushed it hard. It tottered backwards and fell into the mud. But it would be back. Oh, it would be back. These things took a licking and kept on ticking.

Flashlight in hand, Giles had been trying for some time to get one of his books out of his canvas sack to look for a spell or something to re-dead the undead. But the zombies kept coming too fast for him to complete the mission. He, Willow, and Xander could do only so much damage to the opposition.

Could anyone around here spell Alamo?

"Look!" Willow cried, pointing. "There's a little space between them. If we can get to the top of that crypt—"

Xander glanced in the direction of her outstretched finger and pushed her to the side as a zombie tried to chomp down on it. He smacked the zombie in the face with the crossbow. It slipped on the wet grass and crashed to the earth.

"Thanks," Willow said. "Look, see how we've mowed down a path?"

He did see. Somehow, the three of them had thinned the zombies in a fairly clear line from where they stood now to a standing crypt, which Giles had once told him was also called a vault. If they could vault onto it, maybe Giles would have enough time to save the day.

That is, if Giles could find the secret ingredients in his magickal recipe file.

"Should we go for it?" Xander asked Giles, rubbing his hands together in anticipation.

"Yes," Giles said. He turned off the flashlight and put it in his sack. The weak moonlight made his face look as gray as a zombie's, a majorly upsetting visual. "Willow, take Buffy's Slayer's bag. I'll carry my sack. Xander, get the crossbow."

Xander put the crossbow under his arm. Then he bent low and cried, "One, two, three, hike!" He barreled in front of Willow and began knocking zombies over like a linebacker. He was afraid of falling, but he was more afraid of being dinner.

"We're right behind you, Xander," Willow said.

Xander got to the vault, kicking a zombie out of his way as Willow joined him. Giles brought up the rear. He threw his sack onto the top of the vault. Xander and Willow did the same.

Then Giles laced his fingers together and stooped. His hair was plastered to his head. He said, "Willow, go first."

She put her foot into his interlaced fingers. Xander held her around the waist. She turned her head and seemed about to say something to him, then looked at him through the buckets of rain for a few seconds and sighed.

She said, "Go."

Giles and Xander hoisted her up. She grabbed on to the stone overhang of the vault's roof and shinnied the rest of the way up and onto the top.

"Xander, go next," Giles ordered.

"No, you go," Xander insisted. When Giles hesitated, Xander said, "You're the only one who can stop these guys permanently."

"Xander, do not argue with me. I'm your school librarian," Giles said, as if that carried any weight.

"Oooh, the voice of authority speaks," Xander said.

Giles rolled his eyes. "As the Watcher, then."

The zombies began to close in. Xander knew it was a waste of time—in more ways than one—to argue with the man. He smacked a zombie in a nice green dress, then realized the shimmering green color of the dress was slime. He put his foot in Giles's handhold, and pushed himself to the top of the vault. Then he rolled onto his stomach and held out his hands for Giles.

A zombie dressed in a policeman's uniform grabbed Giles around the neck. Willow shouted, "No!"

Xander found a broken stone angel resting on its side and wound up for the pitch. He hurled it at the zombie formerly known as cop, connecting with its head. The zombie collapsed to the ground, and Giles climbed up the slippery side of the vault, until Willow and Xander grabbed his hands.

"Heave, heave!" Xander shouted.

"Xander, how can you keep joking at a time like this?" Willow demanded.

"Because if I don't, I'll be visiting Screamland," he confessed, and they hoisted Giles the rest of the way.

"I shall never understand the humor of the American adolescent. Or the American adult, for that matter," Giles said, scrabbling to grab his sack. He pulled out the journal of Timothy Cassidy and began paging, hunching over to shelter the book from the rain.

"Um, Giles, shouldn't you look through *Magickal Realms* for an anti-zombie reversomatic spell?" Willow queried, looking nervously at Xander. Xander nodded at her.

"Will's right," he said. "Isn't she?"

"Here's my thinking," Giles said as he searched through the book. "Samhain is considered the spirit of Halloween, the king of the dead souls who haunt the land of the living. What are zombies but dead souls? His minions? His slaves?"

"One man's perspective," Xander said slowly. "And the correct thing to do with that input is?"

"Mr. Cassidy has written down a spell to deny the power of Samhain over the dead." He kept paging. "Ah, yes, here it is. He calls it the 'Hymn of Orpheus.'" Giles paused and cocked his head. "I rather like that. Orpheus, of course, being the man who—"

"Please, Giles, just do it!" Xander said.

"Yes, yes, of course." Giles cleared his throat and read:

"'King of the Dead, your sway over these forsaken ones is now ended. Begone, animating spirit which moveth limbs most justly frozen!'"

He made a strange sign in the air.

Xander whispered, "Behold the mark of Zorro!"

Willow smacked his arm.

"'Begone, animating demon which setteth upon these souls hungers most unnatural.'"

The zombies began to gasp.

"'Release them from their torment and return their souls to God!'"

They stopped moving.

They stared at one another with eyes that blinked once, twice . . .

Xander distinctly heard one of them murmur, "Glenn, my brother."

And then they fell to the ground and crumbled into dust.

Xander blinked and leaned over the edge of the vault. Willow joined him. Xander put his arm around Giles. "Strong work, Englishman," he murmured.

Giles didn't answer.

Xander and Willow turned to see that he had gotten a stick out of his canvas sack. Giles said, "I believe there are matches in the Slayer's bag, are there not?"

"There areth," Xander said. He picked up Buffy's bag and rummaged through it. "Behold, that which lighteth."

"Giles, what are you doing?" Willow asked.

"Right," Giles said, as Xander found the matches and tossed them to him. "Here."

He handed each of them a bulb of garlic and a few plant leaves. "These are garlic and angelica. Garlic I know you're familiar with. Angelica's quite another matter. It's also called henbane, insane root, fetid nightshade, even poison tobacco, which I find to be a redundant term if there ever was one."

"Yeah, okay, and it's repetitive too," Xander said, trying to hurry Giles up.

"Highly poisonous," Giles went on. "Extremely. It's said the Egyptians used it to assassinate unpopular pharaohs."

Xander looked uncertainly down at his hand. 'And we are doing what with it?"

Giles gestured to the four sticks. "Smear it and the garlic over the tip of the yew ward."

"Smear? Ward? Um, this looks like a stick," Xander said.

"A ward is something that protects you from evil," Willow said quietly, as she took the supplies from Giles.

Xander caught Willow's wrist. "I thought that was a warden. And I thought you just told us this stuff will kill us in fifteen minutes."

"No, we're fine," Giles said distractedly. "Xander, please, just do as I ask this one time."

Miffed, Xander took the garlic and angelica as well and, imitating Giles, began to rub them all over the sticks. "And we are doing this why?"

"According to Cassidy," Giles said, tapping the journal, "we need to light these on fire with candle wax to illuminate our dark way, and then we need the juice of an apple to remind us of the sins of mankind, to preserve our relationship with good," Giles went on, as if he were reciting a grocery list. "These will protect us from Samhain. I hope," he added under his breath. "It worked for Timothy Cassidy."

"The juice from an apple?" Willow said slowly.

"Right." Giles smelled his hand. "Has a pungent odor, wouldn't you say?"

"I would say," Xander said breathily. "Okay, Teach, let's review the material. Now that the zombies are history, and we busy bees are smearing stinky poison stuff on tree branches, and Buffy is on a field trip with the big demon on campus, we are not getting in the car and driving the long, possibly safer, way to the other side of the field, are we?"

Giles looked surprised. "But Xander, that's an excellent suggestion. Why would we not?"

Willow smiled sadly at Xander. "Because we know, since we both grew up here, that there's an apple orchard not far from where we stand." She gestured with her head toward the field. "Right over there."

"Oh, good," Giles said excitedly. "Then we must go. We can complete our wards with the apples from the trees."

"Except there's a barrier there, isn't there?" Willow asked.

"We'll see, won't we?" Giles replied. "First, let's drip the candle wax onto the wards." He gestured toward Buffy's Slayer's bag, which Willow had by her side. "I believe there are candles among Buffy's equipment."

There were. A match flared in the darkness and cast yellow shadows on Giles's face. Xander watched as Giles pulled out a candle and began to mumble things in his Ghostbuster language of choice, which was Latin.

The stink of sulfur cut the scent of the plants as

Giles began to drip the wax onto the sticks. He finished coating the first one and handed it to Willow. He coated another one and gave it to Xander, then made the other two.

"Waxing our wards," Xander said. "Oh, to be in Malibu, waxing our boards."

As soon as all four were coated, Giles hopped off the vault and hurried to the wall. Without a moment's hesitation, he crossed from the wall into the field.

"We are permitted," he said.

Xander looked at Willow. "Much joy," he whispered. "Samhain is letting us in."

"It *is* much joy. We have to save Buffy," Willow said urgently.

"That'll be a first." Xander smiled at her. "Us saving her. Don't worry, Will. You know I'm in on any crazy prank that has to do with Halloween and a violent demise of my person."

She squeezed his hand. "My hero," she said, and he almost believed that she meant it.

He got down off the vault. Willow scrambled down after him.

"After you, m'dear," he said, bowing low, and she carried the Slayer's satchel toward the wall, climbed onto it, and hopped into the field.

"We're here," she said nervously.

"Let me light your wards," Giles said. "They'll offer partial protection until we make it to the orchard."

Then he set theirs on fire.

"We must hurry. Samhain will detect our presence. And as we aren't fully protected . . ." Giles trailed off, looking uncomfortable, then shrugged.

"What?" Xander asked anxiously.

"Nothing," Giles said.

"There's a rift in the Force," Willow said, staring at Giles. "You think Buffy's—you aren't sure this is going to work."

Giles looked at both of them very seriously. "That's correct. I'm not sure. I can't ask you to risk your lives without telling you that. We may fail."

Willow and Xander were silent for a moment. Then Willow raised her chin and said, "Lead on, Macduff."

"And McDonald's, too," Xander said, nodding. "Let's hit those happy trails."

The rain did not let up as they hurried into the orchard. "Smear all the wards with the juice of apples," Giles said. "I have sigils to draw."

"Squiggles?" Willow repeated.

"Sacred symbols," Giles said. "They'll—"

He stopped speaking as something crashed, shrieking, into the orchard. The three froze and stared at one another.

Willow said hopefully, "Buffy?"

CHAPTER 10

The rain came down even harder. The field was already saturated from the earlier storm, and the ground was muddy in spots. Buffy knew she should be careful. She might turn an ankle, even break something, if she didn't slow down.

She didn't slow down.

A broken ankle held no fear for her, not after looking into the flaming eyes of the pumpkin king, the spirit of Halloween. It was as if Samhain was fear itself. Being near him gave her the most monster wiggins in history. All she wanted to do was escape.

Her ragged, bloodstained blouse and black shorts were soaked. Her now-ragged boots punched the muddy ground, splashing when there was a puddle to splash in. Maybe someone else would have fallen, but Buffy was the Slayer. The Slayer was agile. Buffy was—

On her butt in mud. Covered with it. Wanting desperately to make a joke, a snide comment, a wry observation.

No. Nada. Nyet.

There was nothing funny. She didn't even have time to be humiliated by her fall. She got to her knees and glanced back down the hill toward the barn.

"Oh, God, keep him away," she whispered, terrified, though her fear had diminished slightly as she moved up the hill.

In the darkness in front of the barn, she couldn't make out his body at all, couldn't see his shape. But she could see the face. The green flame spurting from the eyes and mouth of his rotting pumpkin head. She had to fight the urge to throw up.

Buffy stood quickly and started up the hill again. She didn't go any slower, but she stared at the ground in front of her, trying to look out for muddy spots.

Then she was in the orchard, darting through the trees, arms up to keep branches from whipping her in the face. She squinted, trying to see through the darkness ahead, and realized she'd have to go through the pumpkin patch again. Still, pumpkins she was sure she could handle. Leap over them or outrun them. They couldn't do her any real damage.

But there was that magickal barrier still to be dealt with. She couldn't keep evading Samhain until dawn. And who was to say he'd even be gone at dawn? It wasn't as if he were a vampire.

Buffy crashed through the orchard, not caring about the noise she was making. She didn't even turn around to see if Samhain was chasing her now. Even if she could see the demon through the trees, she didn't want to. Ever again.

"Sssslayer," his voice whispered nearby, playfully.

She started, eyes darting side to side in search of him. But it was a trick. He was still behind her. But in pursuit, she was sure. He would never let her out of the field alive.

Branches snapped and apples thumped to the ground as she ran on. Her lungs sucked air in greedily, and her breath came in ragged gasps. Then she heard another soft voice.

"Buffy?"

Stunned, she stared up the hill through the trees. The night was pitch black, the rain whipped through the trees, a staccato patter on the leaves. But even through night and rain and orchard, she could see three burning points of light ahead. White-orange flame, not green.

Not Samhain.

"Willow?" she cried. "Xander? Giles?"

"Buffy?" A different voice this time. Giles.

Then she burst from the orchard on the hill and saw them, just a few yards off to the right. They looked almost comical to her, soaked with rain, hair plastered to their heads and faces, holding the thinnest, wimpiest looking torches she'd ever seen. She might have smiled. But she couldn't, for their presence only added to her nausea.

"No, no, no!" she shouted. "I told you guys not to come in here! Majorly bad move, people. Now move it! He's right behind me!"

As if on cue, they heard a crashing through the orchard. Still far down the hill, but they only had a minute or two before Samhain caught up to them.

"He?" Giles asked, obviously unnerved. "Then I was right? It's—"

"Samhain, yeah, and he's very strong, very scary, very unhappy with the Slayer, and anybody who happens to be her bud," Buffy said. "So move it."

"We're not going anywhere," Xander said. "Even if we weren't all trapped in here, which we are, which is bad, we're not running out on you."

"Right," Willow agreed.

"Hear, hear," Giles concurred.

The crashing through the orchard grew louder.

"How are those torches burning in the rain?" she asked.

"Magic," Giles replied. "We've got a great deal of magic to do, I'm afraid. You see, in all this chaos, I have come up with a plan."

"Plan? Good. Go. Quick. Talk. Speak," Buffy babbled, taking a terrified glance over her shoulder.

"These yew sticks are specially treated. They're wards, which will protect us from the dead and from the spirit of Halloween, but unless we want to beat him to death with them, they won't really harm him," Giles said.

"Good. Then we can just sit around until morning," Buffy said happily.

"They'll burn out before then," Giles said apologetically. "We've got to destroy his physical form to stop him. At the very least. The Watcher Cassidy wrote that Erin Randall used fire for that purpose. Which means we've got to trap Samhain and burn the scarecrow inside which he has taken up residence. There are symbols we can use to trap him, but we don't have time for a circle of them, and there's still the matter of the burning."

"Sssslayer! I'm coming for you and for your friends. I haven't eaten a Watcher's heart in four hundred years," Samhain whispered on the wind, his voice echoing in the hiss of the rainstorm.

"Oh my," Giles murmured worriedly, and pushed his glasses up.

Buffy grabbed her Slayer's bag from Xander, glanced once at the canvas sack that Giles had brought, then rummaged through her bag until she came up with what she'd been searching for.

"A weapon?" Willow asked hopefully.

"Absolutely. Lilac Breeze," Buffy replied, holding up a tube of lipstick.

"You keep your lipstick in your Slayer's bag?" Giles asked, appalled.

"Well," Xander said, jumping to her defense, "a fashionable Slayer has to be prepared for anything. Right, Buffy?"

"So right. Giles, show me these symbols," Buffy said.

Giles held up a thin book. On the cover were the words, The Journal of Timothy Cassidy, Watcher.

He opened it, and showed her a page of crudely etched designs. Sigils, Giles said they were.

Buffy hefted her bag, slung it over her shoulder, and looked up. The crashing in the orchard had stopped.

"There's a barn down there," she said softly. "Maybe it's too wet to burn, I don't know. But I'll bet it's full of nice, dry, fire-lovin' hay."

Giles's eyes lit up. In that moment, they connected as Watcher and Slayer. Mutual respect, parallel thoughts. She could tell he knew exactly what she was going to suggest.

Which was good, because that was the moment Samhain chose to make his grand entrance.

The spirit of Halloween erupted from the orchard, razor-straw fingers reaching for Buffy's throat, pumpkin fangs gnashing for her blood. She leaped out of the way as Willow shrieked in horror, and Buffy knew that they were all experiencing the same terror that was lancing through her. It was as if she were being electrocuted with fear.

"Buffy!" Xander called, and she glanced up in time to see him throw her crossbow toward her.

Even as she caught it, Buffy knew it wouldn't do much more than buy her time, but time was exactly what she needed.

"*Ah, Ssslayer,*" Samhain said, as Giles, Willow, and Xander held up the weird ward sticks with the white burning wax on their tips. "*Your friends have come prepared. Well done, Watcher. I see not everyone has forgotten me.*"

"For Timothy Cassidy and Erin Randall, we'll all see you destroyed, pumpkin king!" Giles roared bravely.

Buffy was proud of him.

Samhain was not psyched.

"How dare you call me that! I am no mere gourd, I am the demon lord of all fear, of Samhuinn, of Halloween itself!" Samhain barked angrily. *"Your little sticks will not burn for long. Then I'll taste all your hearts."*

The rotted face turned to stare at Buffy with flaming green eyes.

"But you, Slayer, have no protection," those snapping pumpkin jaws whispered.

"Hello," Buffy said, pushing away her fear for the sake of her friends. "Blind much?" she asked. She lifted the crossbow and fired a bolt right through the rotten pumpkin forehead. It passed all the way through Samhain's head and left a gouting hole of fire behind.

The dark lord of Halloween grunted and took two steps backwards before lifting his hurting, burning head. Buffy paid no attention. The moment she'd fired on him, Buffy tossed the crossbow on the ground near Xander—obviously it wasn't going to stop him—and crashed back through the orchard.

"Tag, you're it!" she called mockingly to Samhain.

"I'll be back for you when the fire burns low, Watcher. You and your friends," Buffy heard Samhain threaten.

Then he thundered after her.

Buffy only hoped that she could beat him to the barn a second time. She realized that even one hundred years earlier, when the horrors of real life had not yet begun to overshadow the horrors of legend and superstition, she would have probably been dead already. But this Samhain was far weaker even than he'd been the last time he'd faced a Slayer.

"Just keep telling yourself that," she grunted as her boots splattered mud to either side.

It seemed only seconds before she burst from the orchard further down the hill and began to sprint through the rain. She prayed, really prayed, that she would not slip again. This time, a fall would mean her death, and the deaths of the others as well.

"Sssslayer!" Samhain hissed behind her. *"The chase is becoming tiresome."*

The barn loomed ahead, huge sliding doors wide open. Buffy didn't even slow this time, just barreled straight inside and headed for the ladder that went up to the hayloft above. She scrambled up to the loft as fast as she could, then turned and pulled the ladder up after her. If not for the prodigious strength that her calling as Slayer gave her, she would never have been able to do it.

She ducked into the hay just as Samhain came in after her.

"I ssssee you, girl," he hissed. *"This time, I see you, hiding there in the hay. My eyes are everywhere on this night."*

Buffy spun and saw it. On the sill of the huge window from which hay was lowered on pulley and cable, the window that looked down on the orchard and the field, sat a carved jack-o'-lantern.

It didn't move. Not this one. But it stared at her.

Then it said, *"I seeeee you!"* in Samhain's voice.

Buffy felt the fear creeping up on her again, spreading through her entire body. She was freezing up with terror, and she couldn't afford that. There was a sudden shudder beneath her, and she heard scratching and sliding and knew that Samhain was climbing the post at the center of the loft, climbing to reach her. To eat her heart. To slay a Slayer.

"No!" Buffy screamed.

She jumped up, ran to the window, and kicked the pumpkin, caving in its face as it tumbled out of the barn. She glanced at the big entry doors and saw that Giles had arrived there. Willow and Xander stood behind him, holding the flaming wards. Buffy thought she could smell apples and garlic, a weird combination, especially considering her fear and the strong smell of the hay. But it wasn't the worst thing that had ever happened to her.

That was climbing up to the loft.

Giles was using one of her vampire stakes to draw in the dirt entry of the barn, sealing the massive doors with powerful magickal symbols. Buffy remembered the designs from the journal very well, had memorized them for one specific reason.

She reached into her pocket and pulled out her Lilac Breeze lipstick. Her favorite, at least this week, but it would go to a good cause. Namely, saving all their lives. She pulled off the top of the tube, and started to draw on the windowsill, re-creating the symbols as best she could remember.

"Now, Slayer," the king of Halloween whispered behind her. *"You've nowhere left to run. Turn and face me."*

Buffy turned, dropping the lipstick. Last stop, everybody off.

"I'm assuming you know your face is on fire," she said, her throat dry, voice cracking with fear. "But were you aware that so is the barn?"

The horrid, sickening, burning smile dripped blood as it grew wider. She was certain that he would merely laugh at her, then step forward and tear her head from her neck with those razor straw hands. But the flames were rising up the walls of the barn now—Willow and Xander had done their job—and the roar of the fire was clearly audible.

Samhain turned to see the barn ablaze.

"Watcher!" Samhain screamed. *"You're next!"*

Buffy shuddered almost uncontrollably at his booming voice, the fear infecting her. It came off him in waves. Her hands shook, her teeth chattered, and she winced and shrank away from him, even though he hadn't come any nearer.

"That's it," Buffy whispered. "I'm outta here."

She turned, stepped onto the windowsill, careful not to smear the lipstick symbol, and with Samhain roaring furiously behind her, Buffy leaped out into the air, forty feet above the ground.

Anyone else would have been killed, or at least

have had numerous shattered bones. Sometimes being the Slayer had its advantages.

"Uhnnffff!" she grunted as she hit the mud and rolled.

Willow was there next to her a moment later, and Giles stood above her, offering a hand to help her up. Xander was a few yards away, still working his way around the barn with his yew ward, or torch, or whatever. She didn't know how Giles had come up with the things, but she was glad he had. Otherwise they'd be dead now.

"Ssssslayer!" Samhain screamed from the window above. His rage was obvious. He was trapped, about to be burned to nothing along with the old barn.

"It isn't over! I'll be back next year, and I won't give you any warning next time. No games. Just your death! Year after year after year until I've tasted your lifeblood, eaten your heart and soul!"

Buffy shivered, turned to Giles, and hugged him. Willow put her hands over her ears.

"She's not listening to you, Great Pumpkin!" Xander shouted. "You are so toast!"

"Over," Willow agreed, and looked at Buffy.

Buffy frowned.

"I don't like that look," Willow said. "I know that look."

"Giles?" Buffy said. "What's he talking about? I thought if we torched him, he'd, y'know . . . scarecrow, fire? As in, finito completo?"

Giles sighed, reached two fingers under his glasses to rub the smoke from his eyes.

"I'm afraid not, Buffy. He's telling the truth. Unless we can trap the spirit, the actual demon Samhain, into that scarecrow body, destroying it will only stop him for this year. He'll be free to come at you again someday," Giles explained apologetically. "But we'll be better prepared next time. We hadn't any idea what we were facing, but now that we do, we will be ready. And one must remember that he gets weaker as the years pass and faith in his power withers."

Buffy stared at Giles. Then she glanced up at the window of the burning barn, where the green flames of the laughing pumpkin mouth were still blazing, mocking her. Threatening gleefully.

"We are not pressing pause," she said, determined. "We are pushing the stop button."

The Slayer held out her hand. "Xander, give me your Swiss Army knife."

Xander pulled the requested multi-purpose and much-valued had-it-since-third-grade knife from his pocket and reluctantly handed it over.

"Giles, give me the ward thingy," Buffy demanded, and held out her other hand.

"What are you going to do?" Giles asked.

"If this magic is a ward, a kind of barrier for him, do you think it'll trap him in that scarecrow body, kind of pin him in there?" she asked.

"Well, there is a certain logic to that, but there's no way to know that. You're just guessing!" Giles snapped. Clearly he was grasping her plan. And not liking it, because blazing infernos and really pissed-off demons were not healthy for Slayers and other living things.

"Uh, Buffy, going back in there would be an extreme lock-me-up-for-my-own-good, okay? Just wanted to get that straight," Xander babbled.

"Buffy," Willow said quietly. "Please don't."

They didn't want her to do it. Buffy didn't want to do it, either. The fear was still there. Samhain wasn't gone yet, the scarecrow body not destroyed. Her stomach churned and she chewed her lip, fighting off the terror.

The yew stick was thin enough, but too long. She sawed the back end of it off, then used the knife to whittle a point on the wax-coated, burning end. Her fingers got a little singed, but the magickal flame did not go out.

"How much time do I have before this thing is useless?" she asked. "How will I know?"

Giles shrugged. "When the fire goes out, you'll know," he said. "I'm sorry I can't do better than that."

Buffy finished whittling, stared hard at Giles. "You've done great, Giles. Saved my life. A lot of lives, probably. I wanted to run away tonight. I did run away. I let you down—"

"Never—" Giles began, but Buffy went on.

"I'm not going to run again. Not ever," she vowed. "I'm the Slayer. No matter what. You've never told me how long you expect me to live, but you have told me I have a duty. I'm going to honor that, Giles."

Buffy picked up the crossbow, which Xander had

carried down from the orchard, and slotted the sharpened yew stick into the weapon. It was larger than the bolts the crossbow usually took, and not totally straight, but it would do.

It had to.

She turned and marched into the burning barn. When the others called after her, she pretended not to hear.

Samhain stood, burning, at the edge of the hayloft and looked down at her with fury. The entire loft was in flames and would probably come crashing down any second. It didn't matter. The demon had to be destroyed forever. She wasn't even certain that her plan would work. But she had to try.

"I knew you'd come back," Samhain roared, his voice penetrating the deafening crackle of the inferno around them. *"No true Slayer could walk away from this final confrontation. That's why Erin Randall died more than four hundred years ago, and why you will die now!"*

Screeching, trailing fire, parts of his scarecrow body dropping to the floor of the barn, Samhain launched himself from the hayloft. Straw claws lashed at Buffy.

Buffy tried to get the crossbow up in time, but she was too slow. The smoke was heavy, her eyes were tearing, and Samhain dropped in front of her, slashing her face and arms with razor-sharp straw fingers. She dropped the crossbow.

Blood ran from the cuts on her forehead. She didn't know how deep they were, but she didn't want to know just now. There was blood on her arms as well. The Slayer ignored them.

She retreated a way across the barn, and Samhain gave chase. He was burning, falling apart, and he had little time in which he could still use his body to destroy her. The problem was, Buffy had exactly the same amount of time in which to destroy him before he was freed by his own destruction, freed to return in another year.

"Ssssad in a way, to see you die. But that's the wonderful thing about Slayers," Samhain hissed. *"There's always a Chosen One."*

"That's right," Buffy sneered. "Crunch all you want, we'll make more."

He lunged at her. Buffy sidestepped the raking claws; she kicked at the arm and it separated from Samhain's body at the elbow. Flaming straw and clothing landed at her feet.

The pumpkin king hissed and went for her again, green flame within the pumpkin head, green fire burning inside the orange. Buffy dropped to her hands and kicked at his scarecrow knee. With the crackling pop of a blazing log, the knee buckled, burning embers flying.

Buffy had hoped Samhain would fall. He did not. The pumpkin that was his face blackened and bubbled. One half of his head was caved in, green flame diminishing.

"You're fast, little girl," the demon sneered. *"Destroy this body, die here in the barn with me, burned alive. I'll still come back."*

Buffy stared at him, the fear threatening to overwhelm her again. She pushed it away, determined. The loft crashed down and she turned her eyes away, held up a hand to block the burning wood and hay that flew into the air.

Samhain came for her then, dragging his ruined leg, but still fast. Buffy was faster. She leaped over him as he dove for her, flipped in the air, and landed in a crouch right next to her crossbow, which was hidden from his view by a piece of charred wood.

The pumpkin king, the demon lord of Samhuinn, roared with pleasure and the pain of his burning host form. But he was triumphant. He would return. And to kill Buffy, all he had to do was keep her inside the barn. She could hear the burning beams above begin to crack and buckle.

"Die with me, Slayer," he whispered.

"Ever the romantic," Buffy snarled, and aimed the crossbow at the scarecrow's chest.

The remaining pumpkin eye widened as Samhain saw the magickal flame which still burned at the end of her crossbow bolt, saw the white candle wax, and knew what it was she had planned.

"Trick or treat," Buffy said grimly.

She pulled the trigger; the bolt flew impossibly straight and true and embedded itself in Samhain's chest.

"Noooooooo!" the demon screamed, and grabbed for the end of the shaft with his remaining claw, but could not remove it.

She heard the screeching of the ceiling giving way,

and ran for the open doors. Just as the whole inferno collapsed in on itself, she dove over the symbol Giles had etched in the dirt, rolling to safety, choking on the smoke she'd inhaled, soot on her face.

Buffy lay on the ground, staring at the fire, listening to the king of Halloween scream in fury and pain. Giles, Xander, and Willow helped her to her feet and she leaned on them as they moved a safer distance from the burning barn.

"Whoa, pyromania," Xander said in an awed voice.

"I'm not sure how we shall explain this to the owner of this place," Giles said.

"Wait, uh-uh," Buffy replied, grabbed Giles and Willow by the hand, and began dragging them away. Xander followed.

"Buffy, what are you doing?" Giles asked. "We cannot simply leave."

"Sure we can!" Buffy said, then went into another fit of coughs.

"Can," Xander agreed.

"Have to," Willow added.

"I've been branded an arsonist once already, Giles," Buffy snapped. "That's why my mom and I moved here to the Hellmouth, remember? I'd rather avoid another police investigation."

"Absolutely," Willow agreed. "I mean, you live in the mouth of hell. If you got caught again, I'd hate to think where you'd end up next time."

"Indeed," Giles remarked thoughtfully, then turned to Buffy.

"Well, Miss Summers," he said. "I suppose you've learned a lesson this evening, yes? Perhaps you'll think twice in the future before complaining about a lull in the Slaying business."

They all stared at him.

Buffy was the first to laugh.

It felt good.

About the Authors

Christopher Golden's novels include the vampire epics *Of Saints and Shadows* and *Angel Souls & Devil Hearts;* the best-selling trilogy *X-Men: Mutant Empire*, featuring the world-famous Marvel Comics characters; *Hellboy: The Lost Army;* and the new hardcover *Battlestar Galactica* novel, *Armageddon*, which he co-authored with actor Richard Hatch.

Christopher is the regular writer on the best-selling comic book series *Shi*, from Crusade Entertainment, and his own *Facelift*, from Caliber. He has also worked on such comic book titles as *Wolverine, X-Man, The Crow, Daredevil/Shi, Spider-Man Unlimited, Blade*, and *Vampirella*.

He was born and raised in Massachusetts, where he still lives with his wife, Connie, and their sons, Nicholas and Daniel. He is currently at work on the hardcover novel *X-Men: Codename Wolverine* and the third in his vampiric Shadow Saga, *Of Masques and Martyrs*.

Four-time Bram Stoker Award winner Nancy Holder has sold twenty-three novels, including *Highlander: Measure of a Man*, based on the TV series, and *Dead in the Water*. She has also written over a hundred and fifty short stories; game fiction, most notably for FTL

Games' DungeonMaster series; and TV commercials and comic books in Japan. She has been translated into over two dozen languages.

She dropped out of high school at the age of sixteen to become a ballet dancer in Germany, and eventually went on to graduate from the University of California with a degree in communications. She also lived in Japan for three years.

She currently lives ninety-three miles south of Disneyland (in San Diego) with her husband, Wayne, their daughter, Belle, and their Border collies, Mr. Ron, Maggie, and Dot. In her spare time, she watches the worst horror movies she can find and works out at the gym.

Christopher and Nancy first met over the phone when Christopher bought an essay from Nancy for his Stoker Award–winning collection of horror film essays, *Cut!: Horror Writers on Horror Film*. They met in person two years later in a Chinese food restaurant off Times Square in New York. They wrote this novel via the internet, and are already hard at work on another project together.

"I'm Buffy, and you are history."

BUFFY
THE VAMPIRE
SLAYER™

As long as there have been vampires, there has been the Slayer. One girl in all the world, to find them where they gather and to stop the spread of their evil and the swell of their numbers.

#1 THE HARVEST

A Novelization by Richie Tankersley Cusick

Based on the teleplays by Joss Whedon

Created by Joss Whedon

#2 HALLOWEEN RAIN

Christopher Golden and Nancy Holder

 From Archway Paperbacks
Published by Pocket Books

1399-01